D0952493

THE
THIRTEENTH
HOUR

ALSO BY QUINN SOSNA-SPEAR

The Remarkable Inventions of Walter Mortinson

THE THIRTEENTH HOUR

QUINN SOSNA-SPEAR

Simon & Schuster Books for Young Readers
NEW YORK LONDON TORONTO SYDNEY NEW DELHI

SIMON & SCHUSTER BOOKS FOR YOUNG READERS
An imprint of Simon & Schuster Children's Publishing Division
1230 Avenue of the Americas, New York, New York 10020

SIMON & SCHUSTER BOOKS FOR YOUNG READERS
and related marks are trademarks of Simon & Schuster, Inc.
For information about special discounts for bulk purchases, please contact
Simon & Schuster Special Sales at 1-866-506-1949
or business@simonandschuster.com.
The Simon & Schuster Speakers Bureau can bring authors to your live event.
For more information or to book an event, contact the Simon & Schuster Speakers Bureau at
1-866-248-3049 or visit our website at www.simonspeakers.com.
Interior design by Hilary Zarycky
The text for this book was set in Warnock Pro.
Manufactured in the United States of America
0921 FFG
First Edition
2 4 6 8 10 9 7 5 3 1

Library of Congress Cataloging-in-Publication Data
Names: Sosna-Spear, Quinn, author.
Title: The thirteenth hour / Quinn Sosna-Spear.
Description: First edition. | New York : Simon & Schuster Books for Young Readers, [2021] | Audience: Ages 8-12. | Audience: Grades 4-6. | Summary: When her dying aunt gives her a magical pocket watch, twelve-year-old Rosemary, as she begins to dream, enters a fantastical place where each hour of the watch takes her to a different world--until the class bully steals the watch, and Rosemary must gather the magic from all twelve worlds to rescue a boy she does not even like.
Identifiers: LCCN 2021009637 (print) | LCCN 2021009638 (ebook) | ISBN 9781534451889 (hardcover) | ISBN 9781534451902 (ebook)
Subjects: LCSH: Magic—Juvenile fiction. | Dreams—Juvenile fiction. | Pocket watches—Juvenile fiction. | Aunts—Juvenile fiction. | Friendship—Juvenile fiction. | Rescues—Juvenile fiction. | Adventure stories. | CYAC: Magic—Fiction. | Dreams—Fiction. | Clocks and watches—Fiction. | Aunts—Fiction. | Friendship—Fiction. | Adventure and adventurers—Fiction. | LCGFT: Action and adventure fiction.
Classification: LCC PZ7.1.S682 Th 2021 (print) | LCC PZ7.1.S682 (ebook) | DDC [Fic]—dc23
LC record available at https://lccn.loc.gov/2021009637
LC ebook record available at https://lccn.loc.gov/2021009638

When I was eleven years old, I wrote my very first book. It was a picture book. (You will notice that there are no pictures in this book. This makes sense, as the pictures in that book were not very good.)

My fifth-grade teacher, Mrs. Spracher, thought the book was wonderful, however.

She pulled me aside and told me, "Quinn, you're going to write books one day. The first one you should dedicate to your parents, but you're going to dedicate the second one to me."

So, Janis, I'm proud to say that this one is for you.

And for any readers, I need to tell you something. If you want to write a book, you can. All you have to do is try. One day, in fact, you will write a book. That one you should dedicate to your parents.

The second one, though? You dedicate that one to me.

THE WORLD INSIDE THE WATCH

Magic does exist, but only we know how to reach it."

That's what my aunt Jo used to tell me as I was falling asleep on her couch when I was younger. The fireplace was warm and crackled, her blankets were soft and heavy, and her hands would scratch through my hair as she whispered—only for me to hear.

"You see, Rose, there's a place where anything is possible, and when you go there, you will become more powerful than anyone you've ever met."

"Me? But I'm small."

"That doesn't matter when you have magic, does it?"

"How do I get there?" I'd ask, although I already knew the answer.

"You use the watch, of course." Jo would pull the long

gold chain from her pocket slowly, link by link, until the pocket watch came into view.

It was perfectly round, and the gold was as bright as the fire in the hearth. On the top was a loop, attached to which was a thin gold chain with braided links. Next to the loop was a button. Jo pressed it, and the sides, separated into twelve petals, fell open like a flower.

Pictures were carved on the back of each segment of the gold shell. They depicted magical landscapes that could exist only in Jo's fantasy world. In the middle was the clock, with long bronze hands that ticked silently.

The first time she showed me, my hand reached out on its own, and Jo clicked it shut.

Only Jo was allowed to touch the pocket watch.

"It's not yours yet, my love—but one day it will be, and then you will hold the key that will allow you to enter the other world."

"When can I go?"

"When I'm ready to give it to you," she'd say.

I knew all twelve realms inside the watch by heart. Jo had told me about her adventures in them and had painted me dozens of pictures.

In Ten O'Clock you turned into an animal to escape the giant flowers that followed you. Jo said she was a mink there, which she explained was a lot like if a snake and a hamster had a baby. I wasn't sure I wanted to be a mink. She thought I might be a fox. I always liked foxes after that.

Then in Eleven O'Clock you could create anything you could think of just by drawing it. If you wanted your own pet dragon, all you had to do was learn to draw one. But you had to be careful, because once it was created, the dragon would take on a life of its own. It might bite you or singe off your eyebrows.

But Jo didn't just tell me about the magic, even though that was the fun part—she also told me about the dangers. You had to be extra careful in the magical clock world, because whenever something is that amazing . . . there must always be something about it that's equally frightening.

"And it will be your job, Rosey-Posey, to save it one day."

"Why me?"

"Because I'm too old and because you're the perfect mix of smart, kind, and *special*."

That was always the best part of Jo's stories, when she told me I was special. No one else believed that, and so I would listen to her as she scratched my head, and drew pictures for me, and gave me lessons on how to survive in the magical realms.

I stayed awake for hours more than I would any

other night, just to hide in her stories for a little longer. She even had a book about the world.

The book was encased in red leather and bound with gold thread. The title was carved in cursive writing that I had thought was just perfect. The middle of the letters were gold as well, chipping only slightly. They read: *The Thirteenth Hour.*

On every page was bright artwork that had been painted with a thin brush.

On the first page was a tall man who had black hair with a puff of white on top, a floppy mustache, and an old-timey tie. His name was Amisi, and he was going on an adventure.

Amisi flew over the clock world carrying a fistful of brightly colored balloons.

I loved that world, because it felt like the exact opposite of the dry deserts of Arizona that I had grown up in, filled with identical white houses with identical pools and identical cactus-shaped WELCOME HOME mats.

As I grew older, though, I realized that the watch world was *just* a book—a story that Jo had read and liked. But I still listened and nodded along, so that I could be special for a little longer too.

When I couldn't keep my eyes open anymore, Jo would recite the ending to me.

Scrawled on the back cover was a painted line of black writing: *To my Mila. I will come back for you once I've saved our true home.*

Then below was the rhyme that Jo had sung to me so many nights when I was little.

"So that you'll remember it always," Jo would whisper.

"*The little girl went off to bed and found a place inside her head. Her eyes closed shut when the clock struck one, and she dreamt she could fly up to the sun. When she awoke the very next day, she couldn't wait to go back and play.*

"*Next she slept, the clock struck two, and she dreamt that she sailed on the ocean blue.*

"'*How fun,*' *she cried at the fire of three,* '*one of these worlds could be made for me!*' *It was not the colorful city of four,* '*but I'll keep going, there might be more.*'

"*She was strong at five and small at six.* '*This must be magic, not just tricks.*' *There's steel, caves, and snow at seven, eight, and nine, but then she worried:* '*Which hour is mine?*' *Not ten's garden, nor eleven's art.* '*It must be the last one,*' *she knew in her heart.*

"*At long last, when the clock struck twelve, she found a kingdom for herself.*"

THE SMOKE KEEPER

Something crawled toward me in the darkness.

My head was filled with fog, and in the pitch-black room I couldn't figure out where I was.

How did I get here? It was hard to think, but I was soon distracted by the scraping sounds of the thing moving. As it came closer, I could finally see what it was.

It's a man, I thought. Sort of, anyway. His arms and legs were too bony inside his bright yellow suit. A top hat shadowed his face. The way he moved, however, didn't look like anyone I had ever seen—he jerked as he pulled himself across the floor toward me.

"Stop," I tried to yell, but it came out as a whisper. My chest was so tight, I couldn't speak.

The man said nothing, but I could hear the scratching of his nails as they dragged across the floor. My chest grew even tighter when I saw the nails. They were long, yellow, and cracked—curling toward his palms like claws.

I tried to run, but my body was frozen—except for my pounding heart.

As the man came nearer, I could finally see his face.

He didn't stare *at* me, he stared *through* me, like an X-ray. But he had no eyes—just dark, empty sockets. His nose was broken, and his lips looked like they had been torn into his face.

The scariest thing, though, was his teeth. They were long, yellow, and cracked, just like his nails. Each tooth was as long as my fingers, and together they kept his mouth pried open, like one of those fish that live at the bottom of the ocean.

The teeth parted for a second—just long enough for a rattling breath to squeeze through, along with glittering gray smoke.

It's a Smoke Keeper! I recognized him now and realized, *This is a dream.*

But even though I knew what he was, as the Smoke Keeper scuttled closer, all elbows, knees, and teeth, I found that I was still afraid.

But it's just a dream, Rose! Wake up!

It was like the more I realized it wasn't real, the faster the man moved.

Wake up! Wake up now!

His mouth spread wide, teeth opening. A wheeze rattled across his lips.

I could hear Jo's voice in my memory. *"All you hear is a long death rattle, and then it's too late."*

Just as he reached me, he whispered, *"Rosemary."*

"Rosemary!"

"Ahh!"

As soon as my body unfroze, I felt like I was falling. I caught myself just in time and realized, *Oops. I'm in class.*

My classmates snickered as they stared at me. I wiped at my cheek and, ugh, yeah, there was *drool*. Blood rushed to my face, causing my cheeks to flush.

I looked up to see Mr. Topinka standing over my desk, his mustache scrunched up in the way it did when he was mad. Mom always said that I should try to make his mustache scrunch up less.

"Sorry, Mr. Topinka. What's the question?"

"Well, my first question is why are you sleeping in my class?"

More people giggled. Someone kicked my chair from behind.

I didn't have to turn around to know it was Jeremiah.

He was super tall, his long legs barely fitting under his desk. He had blond hair that was shaved on the sides and spiked up in a mohawk. His eyes were the same color blue as clear pool water. When he looked at you, it made you shiver because something about his eyes was cold.

He kicked my chair again. I gritted my teeth, ignoring him.

Then his twin sister, Fallon, reached over to hit his arm, and I had to stop myself from smiling. She had the same blond hair and blue eyes, but *her* eyes were warm. She looked at me, then turned away just as fast.

We used to be friends. She stopped hanging out with me last summer when people started making fun of her for it. I don't know what they think is wrong with me, exactly. It's like everyone just decided I was a loser all at the same time. Maybe it was because of my clothes, or because I didn't talk very much, or because I—

"Earth to Ms. Marks."

My eyes shot to the front of the classroom. "Uh, sorry, Mr. Topinka."

"Now, *why* were you sleeping in my class?"

"I don't know."

I didn't want to tell him that the *real* reason I was always tired in class was because I had nightmares at home.

"That's not an answer. But it's fine, you don't have to explain it to me."

I sighed. *Thank goodness.*

"You can, however, explain it to your father. He's here to pick you up." Mr. Topinka stepped aside, revealing the small frame of Mrs. Lamprey, the office aide, behind him. "Mrs. Lamprey will escort you to the office."

My dad was here? But why? He never picks me up, and it was so early . . .

My classmates laughed more as I stumbled to stand.

Aunt Jo always told me that if you looked at Smoke Keepers—at *monsters*—with fear in your eyes, then they would go in for the kill. If they saw fear, then they knew they could win. I know bullies aren't Smoke Keepers, but sometimes they feel like monsters anyway. So I didn't look at the other kids as I followed Mrs. Lamprey.

Because I was looking at the ground, I didn't see the boy who appeared at Mrs. Lamprey's side. I crashed into him and stumbled again. "Oh! Sorry, I—" I mumbled.

I looked up at him. He had long, shaggy black hair and dark brown eyes streaked with gold. I had never seen him before.

"You all right?"

I was surprised by how earnestly he was asking it.

But before I could answer, Mr. Topinka ushered him into the room.

"Oh, and of course! Class, we have a new student. Let's welcome Alejandro Fuentes."

I heard the class shouting their greetings just as the door slammed shut.

THE SECRET GIFT

Wes, my dad, was fed up by the time I got to the office.

"Come on, we're running late."

"Late for what?" I asked, jogging to keep up with him as he strode long dad steps toward the parking lot.

"To see your aunt."

"Aunt Jo?"

He didn't say a word as we climbed into his big truck and pulled out of the parking lot.

It took most people two hours to drive to Phoenix from Globe, where I live. But Wes wasn't like most people—he wasn't even like most dads.

Most dads ask you about how your day was, or put your drawings up on their fridge, or actually, you know, want to spend time with you.

Wes didn't do any of those things, and it took him only one hour to drive to Phoenix. He liked to drive really fast. I figured it was because if he drove fast, then he could spend less time with me.

"Where are we going?" I asked.

"I already told you."

"No, but, like, where *exactly*? Jo's house?"

I glanced at him out of the corner of my eye; it looked like he was deciding whether or not he wanted to lie.

"The hospital," he said finally. "The cancer came back."

I knew Jo had *been* sick, I just didn't realize that she was *still* sick. The last time I saw her was two years ago when I was in the fourth grade. That's when she got diagnosed with brain cancer.

Back then we would take car trips to see Aunt Jo all the time.

Aunt Jo was a loner like me. Mom called her a "hermit." She lived far away from any other houses, walled off by ginormous Aleppo pines. She wasn't married and didn't have any kids. She did have really long hair, though; thick orange hair that she wore in a braid down her back. She was so short and the braid was so long that it reminded me of a tail. *"Minks do have long tails, kid,"* she'd say whenever I'd mention it.

I liked Jo. I liked her mostly because she liked me. Aunt Jo said she thought I was great because I wasn't similar to anyone else. Funny, when it seemed like that was the reason nobody liked me at school.

Jo decided to become my "mentor." She said that a mentor was like a teacher, except a mentor wouldn't mark you tardy or give you grades. She would just teach me things. Jo's the one who taught me to draw and paint.

She said that painting was going to be my strongest magic when I went into the other world. *"The magic of Eleven!"* So I had to practice to prepare.

She told me lots of things, and at the time I didn't think it was weird. I was just happy that someone finally understood me and didn't think I was a total loser. We spent hours in her garage as she gave me art lessons.

She thought it was important that your picture felt real—no, that it *was* real. If you drew a man, then he had to really be thinking things. He had to have a family and had to want something. It was your job to make him alive. *"Otherwise the magic won't work."*

Then she told me about the Smoke Keepers.

"They're called Smoke Keepers because magic looks like smoke, see? They try to steal people's smoke away. Don't let them take it from you, Rose."

Jo drew the Smoke Keepers a lot.

When I told Mom about the whole "Aunt Jo told me that monsters are real and they're trying to steal my magic" thing, it caused a big fight between her and Dad. Mom said that I wasn't allowed to get mentored by Aunt Jo anymore.

I don't know if that's a good or a bad thing. What I do know is that the only person who ever actually liked me for me told me that I should be afraid of everyone.

And now she was sick again. *It must be pretty bad if she's in the hospital . . .*

I shook my head. It would be fine. It had to be fine. She was Jo, and Jo couldn't be taken down by anything or anyone. She was the strongest person I ever knew.

Wes and I drove in silence for a while, which I liked. Wes and I never had much to talk about.

"How's your mom?" he finally asked.

"Fine."

"Still working at that diner?"

I nodded. Mom worked mornings at the diner. She hated it because they made her wear a 1950s dress with red and white stripes. Then at night she went to the community college. She was studying to become a nurse.

"What about you?"

"What about me?" I asked.

"Join any sports?"

"No."

"Any clubs?"

I just shook my head.

"So you're not doing *anything*?"

"Not really," I said. I was still drawing a lot, but I knew that wasn't what he meant. Wes was always worried about college. He said if I wanted to get into Columbia, which is where he went, then I would have to have good grades and "important hobbies."

Drawing didn't count because you couldn't write it on a college application, Wes said.

"Why not? You're not still doing *art* or anything like that, are you?" he asked me, looking away from the road.

He thought it was a waste, that I needed to be spending all the time I wasn't *in* school doing something that would *prepare* me for school. Art was just "fun," and that wasn't good enough. *"You don't get graded in fun,"* he'd chide me.

I paused before answering. "No."

"Good. Well, when the new year starts, I'll find a good club for you. How does debate sound?"

Terrible.

"Okay."

There was no point in arguing with Wes. He was a

lawyer, so he argued for a living. *And I just do art.*

"Good. When you go to law school, debate will be an important skill. It's never too early to think about college, Rosemary."

The hospital was all white and smelled like plastic and medicine. I didn't like it.

Wes and I stood in front of the door labeled 1051. That's the room number the nurse had given us. The door was cracked, and I could hear voices from the inside.

"I told you that I don't want it!" *Jo's voice.*

"Oh, Miss Marks, I promise it will help. Just take it." I peeked my head in to see a nurse standing in front of the bed.

"And I told you to—" Jo's raspy voice was cut off by loud, wet coughs.

The nurse sighed as she stepped away, revealing a thin, pale woman I barely recognized. She was propped up on the white bed by pillows, the covers drawn up to her chin. Her hair was only a bit red now, mixed with mostly white. The most surprising thing, though, was that it was short—just past her ears. Her skin looked looser than it used to. Her eyes were the same, though: a bright, clear green that looked as if they were keeping a secret. Jo had always said she liked my streaky, spotted hazel eyes more than she liked her own. I didn't understand that. Everything about me was boring.

"Will you take it for me?" The nurse held out a little Dixie cup toward Jo. When she jiggled the cup, something inside rattled.

"Fine." Jo pushed down the covers with one hand; in the other she clasped something small and gold. After a moment she set it to her side. I saw just a glimpse of the thing through the folds of the blanket. It was the pocket watch.

The nurse spied it too and became transfixed. "Where did you get—"

But Jo snatched the Dixie cup out of the nurse's hand and tossed the pill into her mouth.

"Now get out!" Jo grabbed the gold watch and shoved it back under the covers.

The nurse shook her head as if shaking off a dream. "All right, well, press the button if you need anything, Miss Marks."

I barely had time to step to the side of the door as the nurse rushed through. She seemed surprised when she saw me and Wes.

"She's a tough cookie, that Miss Marks."

I just nodded. I didn't like how the nurse had been

staring at the watch. It was the same kind of look a dog gives you when it's sitting under the dinner table waiting for scraps to fall.

"Come on, Rosemary."

I straightened my clothes as Wes walked through the door. It had been a long time since we'd seen each other. What if she didn't even remember me? What if I wasn't as special as she always thought I was? What if she didn't like how I'd changed?

"Lollygagging gets you eaten, Rosey-Posey. Get in here already!"

I couldn't help but smile. It was still the same.

I stepped past Wes and saw her, face-on, for the first time in years. Her bright eyes gleamed, warm and magical, even under these horrible hospital lights.

"Hey, Jo."

"Hey, kid."

I walked toward the bed, my hands stuffed deep in my pockets, my feet dragging on the floor.

"Pick up your feet. You don't know who's living in the dirt underneath 'em."

My shoes shot up, too high, as I stepped. I knew it was just one of her stories. *"Bugs are animals too, Rose! I'm good friends with a particular snail in the Tenth Hour!"* Still, it was always easier to listen to Jo than to argue with her. She'd never admit the magic world wasn't real.

"Hello, Joanne." I winced as Wes used her full name. Jo didn't like when people called her that.

"Hello, *Wesley.*"

I smiled. Wes didn't like it when people called him his full name either.

"How are you?" he asked her.

"I'll be better if you give me some alone time with my niece."

I looked from Jo to Wes. He looked like he was about to argue, but he decided against it. He threw up his arms. "Fine. I'll be back in a few."

As he walked out, I heard him muttering to himself about how it was "always the same with her." Then he slammed the door shut.

"Now come closer, I want to show you something," Jo said as soon as Wes had left.

She pulled the watch out from under the covers. I couldn't help but stare at it. It was so perfect that it hardly looked real. *It's just as I remember it.* Mom didn't have anything nice like that. Is that what all fancy jewelry looked like? *No,* I decided. The watch was definitely the nicest thing I had ever seen.

I wanted to grab for it, to hold it. I *needed* it. As I reached out my hand, Jo pulled the watch back. It made me angry, like I wanted to snatch it from her. Then I realized what I was thinking. *That's weird*, I thought, trying to shake off the strange feeling. The watch had a tendency to put you under a spell.

"So it still has a hold on you, huh? That will wear off the more time you spend looking at it."

"Why did you bring it with you here if—"

"Have you been keeping up with your painting and drawing?" she interrupted.

I sighed with frustration. Jo did that a lot. I knew she didn't want to talk about the watch anymore even if I tried.

"Every day," I said. And it was true. I drew and painted as much as I could.

"You any good? I don't even want to bother talking to you if you aren't any good."

I shrugged. I never had been good enough for Jo. *"Still missing something,"* she'd say.

"Paint me something!" she continued, eyes shining.

"With what?" I asked.

"You can't ask me that. This is a competition! If you want to win, you need creativity."

I nodded. This had been a game we'd played when I was little. The one where you're both supposed to draw or paint a picture using the most unusual tools. The weirdest canvas or utensils won. The reason was so that when you were in Eleven O'Clock, you could make magical drawings out of anything. I always lost—partially because Jo was the only judge and she was competitive, but mostly because she was always better than I was.

Maybe she never let me win just because she wanted me to push harder the next time. If that was true, then it worked.

"Ugh." Jo tried to heave herself up in bed, but it looked like it hurt.

"Wait! Don't get up, you're sick."

"You're just saying that so I don't win again. I have to find my tools."

"I'll get you your tools," I said, pushing her shoulder back toward the mattress. "You shouldn't stand, you're in a hospital."

She looked up at me from under her thin eyelashes. "It's the last place I should be, I'll tell you that."

I felt calm again after she said that. She might look sick, but I could see it in her eyes. She didn't *need* to be here. *I knew it. I knew she would be okay.*

I was relieved, though, because even if she was acting like, well, *Jo*, she did lie back down.

"Fine, you go first, then," she said, her voice hoarse.

"What should I use?"

Jo snorted. "Why are you asking me? If you want to win, you need a plan."

I spun around the room, looking. I was excited, actually. I didn't know how long it had been since I'd felt like this—like I could do whatever I wanted. *I can draw a condensation picture on the mirror with my finger— no, too boring. Carve into the wall with a needle? Too dangerous. Finger paint with an IV bag? Too gross.*

Then I realized, taking three big steps back to Jo: her black purse sat on the table beside her. I rummaged through it without asking, knowing what I was looking for. She didn't stop me.

"Interesting choice," she said as I pulled out a package of pink stomach pills. Jo always had them, and, I suspected, these particular pills were probably as old as I was. I then found a small plastic box of Q-tips. I emptied it, snatching a few of the cotton swabs for myself, and filled the box with water. Then I dropped the pills in and crushed them up with a pen cap as they dissolved. Soon the water was bright pink.

"You need that?" I asked, pointing to a white sheet

folded at the end of her bed. Jo shook her head, face blank. I laid it flat on the floor.

"What do you want me to draw?" I asked, already knowing the answer.

"Whatever you think I need."

So I grabbed a Q-tip and stirred my pink paint with it. *Perfect.* I swiped the Q-tip against the sheet, producing a long, pale line. I smiled. *This might actually work.*

But what *did* Jo need?

The lines emerged faster than I could think, still not sure what I was drawing. My mind was stuck on the image of her as I'd entered the room: how small and tired she'd looked, surrounded by the loud machines, washed away by the all-white walls. She wasn't meant to be small, or tired, or washed out. She was big, and loud, and *Jo.* What she needed was to get out of this horrible place. She needed trees, wind, the sounds of birds and running water, and minks. Many, many minks.

I don't how long I painted in silence, scrambling on my hands and knees, but then it was done. A mural of the place I imagined. *Ten O'Clock. Jo's favorite.* It was right there in pastel colors.

Halfway through, I'd gone into the bathroom attached to the room and got some plastic cups, then I'd found some yellow and blue medications in Jo's purse that she said were safe to crush up as well. The mural looked a little messy, I guess, but I hoped it was enough.

I glanced up at Jo, who hadn't said anything the whole time. She was staring at the painting.

"The sheet was thinner than I thought, so the colors bled a little, and I shouldn't have mixed so much water into the pink, but—"

"You win," she said, lowering her blankets to her chest.

"Wait, what?"

She smiled, and for a second I thought she might have little tears in the corners of her eyes. Must have been the lights, though. Jo never cried.

"You win, kid. You're good enough."

"But you didn't get your turn yet!"

"I don't need it. I can already tell."

"But—"

"Before you get your prize, however," she interrupted again, "answer me this: Why do you like to make art?"

"I . . ." I glanced back at the drawing, not sure of the answer myself. "It's the only thing I'm really good at. It makes me feel . . . worth something," I finally admitted, looking up at her. I wouldn't have told anyone but Jo that. Not Mom, not Wes, not *any* of the kids at school, but for some reason I thought Jo might understand. Jo, the hermit everyone judged and no one understood. *No one but me.*

"Good answer. Now, would you like to see your prize?"

"Sure, why not?" I said, unable to imagine what kind of prize she'd find in a boring old hospital room.

Then her hands emerged from the covers along with the gold watch. She held it up but said nothing. I tried not to look at the watch again, afraid of what it might do to me. Instead, I unfocused my eyes, looking only at her face.

"What do you think?" she asked.

"Of what?"

"Your prize."

Wait, what? She was going to give me the watch for smearing pill juice on a bedsheet?

"Are you kidding?"

She shook her head, holding the watch out for me to take, but I didn't dare.

"But," I exhaled, frustrated, "I don't know if this is a joke or if you're just being silly. That watch is worth a lot more than a drawing."

"Rosemary, I have had this watch since I was younger than you. It is the most important thing I own. I have thought long and hard about who I should give it to, and there is no one else. You're the one."

"I am not! *You* should keep it. It's not like you're dying."

"If I was, would you take it?"

The sounds in the room faded away as I looked at her.

"Are you?"

After too long she rolled her eyes. "Not right now, but that's not the point. The point is that I'm giving you a gift and you're being a little slug after years of ignoring me."

The sounds returned as a loud smack in the face.

"Are you . . . sure?" I asked finally, now looking to the watch, which seemed to glitter even more than it had when I'd first seen it.

"I was more sure a few minutes ago."

My fingers rose, grasping for it. Inches before they touched, Jo snatched the watch back into her hand. "First, though, you have to promise me something."

I could feel my heart pounding. I knew there had to be a catch. "What?"

"There are rules to this watch, Rose."

Maybe Jo really was as strange as Mom had always said, or maybe she was just playing with me. "Okay. What are the rules?"

"The first rule is that you never let this watch out of your sight. It stays on you at all times. You never lose it. You never forget it. You never let anyone else touch it. In fact, don't let anyone even *see* it."

I nodded.

"The second rule is that you sleep with the watch. Every night it stays on you. Hold it, lie on it, shove it down your pants, I don't care. Just don't let it be seen."

That was weirder, but the look on Jo's face told me not to ask questions. "Yeah, sure."

"The last thing is that you must fall asleep tonight between eleven and twelve."

"Huh?"

Jo held up her hand, severe. "Don't you *dare* go to bed before eleven or after twelve. If you do, then you have to stay up all night and try again tomorrow. No arguing."

"What are you talking—"

"*No* arguing, Rose. This is very important. And when you do fall asleep, I want you to imagine the waves painted on the inside of the watch—"

I threw up my hands. "Please just tell me this is a joke already."

She clutched the watch tighter to her chest. I was surprised by how angry she looked.

"There's . . . ," she began, her voice trembling, "a *world* inside this watch."

"Jo, I know you made up those stories—"

"I'm *serious*." Her eyes whipped back to me. "Deathly serious. You must be careful with it, Rose. It's important. There's a whole world with people in it. It's *alive*."

"Jo . . . ," I began, my heart thumping with such urgency that I could hear it in my ears. *She can't really think those stories are real, can she?*

"Do you finally get it?"

I nodded. I always thought Jo was just playing with me by pretending the stories about the magical world were real, but if she *really* believed in them, then she must be sicker than I'd ever realized.

"Are you feeling okay? Should I go get someone? Like Wes? Or a nurse?" I asked, my voice shaking.

"No, I need—" Her face looked angry, but then she cut herself off, sucked in a puff of air, and closed her eyes. "All right. I'm sorry. I shouldn't have told it to you like that."

"So it *was* a joke?"

She cringed. "No, it isn't a *joke*. It's my life." My eyes went wide again, and she held up her hands. "I mean," she continued, "it's *that* important to me."

There was a too-long pause as neither of us knew

what to say. Then she broke the silence. "Are you . . . happy, Rose?"

"What do you mean?"

"I mean, are you happy with school? And friends? And the whole *world* around you?"

"Psh," I couldn't help but snort. "That's a silly question."

"Why?"

My hands found their way to my hips. "Well, are you asking if I'm happy that I'm trapped in class all day when all I want to do is draw? Am I happy that everyone thinks I'm weird? Am I happy that I feel like there's no place for me?"

My heart was pumping faster. I don't know why I said all of that, but I think it was just because no one had ever asked me that question before. People almost never *really* wanted to know what I thought.

"No, I'm not happy."

I expected her to yell or get mad, but instead, she nodded. "Me too. When I was your age, Rose, I felt like the whole world was made for everyone else. It was like I wasn't supposed to be born. And yet"—her eyes suddenly looked brighter and her lips curved into a smile—"I found the place where I was meant to be."

She pulled out the watch again, dangling it in front of me. I wanted to believe her.

"Do you want to be happy too, Rose? I'm offering you the key."

"I—" The intensity on her face showed me that she really believed it. Could she be telling the truth?

"The hours. The magic. The monsters. *They're real.* They've always been real, and I just needed you to learn so that you could take over for me. I picked you for a reason."

She thrust the watch toward me, leaning her thin body off the bed.

"I—I—" I couldn't find the words.

"Trust me," she begged.

I tore my gaze from the watch and looked into her eyes.

"I can't."

I started backing away from the bed, toward the door.

"Rose." She stretched her thin arms as far as they would go and grabbed a pocket of my baggy jeans, pulling me into her with her bony fingers. "Please believe me. When have I . . ." Her words became slurred and her mouth dropped.

"Jo?"

Her body went stiff for a moment before softening, her hand falling away from me. I was as still as a statue as I watched her. Her eyes rolled backward into her head, her chest pushed up toward the ceiling, and then her whole body started shaking.

I wasn't thinking after that. My legs just moved on their own, running to the door. I ripped it open and raced down the hall until I found a nurse.

"There's something wrong with my aunt!"

THE LATE-NIGHT CALL

We were stuck at the hospital for hours as the doctors ran tests. They told me that Jo had had a seizure but that she was okay. I told them about all of the . . . weird things she was saying—about how she really believed there was a magical world and stuff—but they didn't look too worried.

I asked if she was really dying, but everyone just told me that she was "stable" right now. I didn't know what they meant by that.

"Then, can she go home?" I'd asked, but no one had answered.

Once all the doctors and nurses had left her room, the sky looked like a bruise outside the vast hospital windows. I asked a lady at the nurse's station if I could say goodbye to Jo, but she wouldn't let me. "You can come back tomorrow, sweetie, when she's rested."

I took one last look at the foggy glass on the door to my aunt's room, seeing the outline of her back facing me. *She doesn't belong here.*

The drive to Wes's house was slow and silent. Neither of us knew what to say.

The second I stepped into the house, I was rushed by a short, blond woman with a big, round belly that pressed hard like a basketball against me as she wrapped me in a hug.

"Oh, Rosemary! Hello!"

Cindy was Wes's wife. She'd been my babysitter when I was little.

"Where's dinner?" Wes yelled from the kitchen.

Cindy let go of me, holding up a finger before shuffling in after him. "In the oven. I didn't want it to get cold!" I watched her go. As soon as she was gone, I heard her whisper-arguing with Wes.

Mom and Wes used to argue like that too. I wondered if Cindy and Wes would get a divorce. I didn't want to go through another divorce, so I hoped that they wouldn't.

I ignored them as I walked into the living room, out of hearing range, and called Mom.

She had agreed to get me my own phone when I turned eleven so that when we were separated, like now, when I was at my dad's, we could still talk. She had called me ten times while I was at the hospital.

"Hello?"

"Rosey!" I pulled the phone away before Mom could bust my eardrum. "How are you? Where are you? Are you okay?"

I walked in big circles around the room as we spoke.

"So, I get this message from your dad, right? But he doesn't call me back! And then you don't call me back. And then, okay, my break ended, but then I called you both again, *and no one calls me back!*"

"Mom?"

"What?"

"Jo's . . . Jo's really sick." My throat closed halfway through, causing me to hiccup the last word with a sob.

"Oh, bubala, tell me all about it."

I explained what had happened. The tears leaked from my eyes even though I tried to plug them back up. By the end I was just able to dry my cheeks and get my voice calm. She asked when I was coming home.

"I don't know," I said, sighing.

"Sorry, my love."

"It's fine," I said, resting my forehead on my hand. I

jumped and pulled the phone from my ear when a loud cowbell rang out from the hallway.

"So Cindy still uses the cowbell, huh?" I heard Mom ask.

"Guess so," I mumbled.

Then I heard Cindy's chipper voice. "Dinner is served!"

Cindy always sounded happy—usually in the worst situations.

Dinner was quiet. I felt uncomfortable eating at the long table. Mom and I usually ate in the living room while watching TV.

After dinner I went to bed. The guest room was decorated in laces, doilies, and decorative plates with paintings of birds on them. I didn't stay with my dad very often, but whenever I did, I was always relegated to the lace-and-doily room. I hated it—I always had the feeling it was haunted by some dusty, old ghost. The blankets smelled stale and felt cold. Even the air seemed like it had gone bad. It just . . . it didn't feel like home.

It's weird when you feel invisible even when you're with your own family. *Maybe* I'm *the dusty, old ghost.*

Cindy popped her head through the doorway. "I know you never want anything special, but I left you some pajamas."

"Oh, wow." I plastered on a smile. They would be too big like always, I knew it. "Thanks, Cindy."

Cindy's face lit up and she hugged me again. "No problem, hon. Let me know if you need anything!" Then she hobbled down the hallway. My fake smile fell. Cindy wasn't mean, but I never really liked her after Mom and Dad got divorced. I liked her before she was my stepmother.

The room was small and dark and weird. *I'm never going to be able to sleep here.* I glanced at the white clock on the wall: 10:15 p.m.

It was going to be a long night. With nothing else to do, I flopped on the short, springy bed.

I looked again at the clock, watching the second hand tick.

10:18 p.m.

What had Jo meant? *"You must fall asleep tonight between eleven and twelve."* Like I could make myself do that even if I wanted to.

And that watch. Would she have really given it to me? I'd wanted to take it, but it felt wrong, like I was stealing an artifact from a museum.

I groaned, rubbing my hands hard against my face. I wished I could take a bath and wash the day off, but I'd probably wake someone up. At the very least I had to get out of these dirty clothes.

I turned to look at the giant, plaid pajamas hanging from the doorknob. The Walmart tag was still attached.

I pulled my sweatshirt over my head and unzipped my jeans, moving fast, worried that someone might walk in. As I kicked them off, something small and cold flew out from one of the pockets. I jumped away, then looked down to see a gold chain. I bent over and pulled it out, the weight of the end heavy. Moments later it was dangling before me, gleaming in the light.

The watch. It's the watch! Jo must have slipped it in there when she grabbed me, and I didn't even . . .

Everything around me melted away. The watch was so glittery, and round, and perfect.

I rubbed a thumb across the surface. Somehow it made no reflections. Maybe it was *too* shiny.

In that instant I was so happy, and I'm not even sure why. Just that this beautiful thing was *mine.* And with that thought, the rest of reality came flooding back.

Jo had given this to me, had even told me that there were *rules.*

Instantly more awake than I had been, I threw on my pajamas, then practically hovered to the bed—never once looking away from my new treasure.

I held it carefully, like it was a delicate egg, rubbing my fingers over its smooth surface. But up close, it looked different from how I remembered it . . . because one of the petals was missing. The one on the very top. *Twelve.* I tried to imagine what the picture on the petal had been, but I couldn't quite recall. The strangeness of that fact didn't worry me, however, because the watch was here. And it was mine.

That's when I faltered. It wasn't really mine, though, was it? It was Jo's. She was just sick and had decided to give it to me while she was tired and on too much medicine.

I felt a burning in my chest as I realized that I should bring it back tomorrow. *She'll be better rested,* I hoped. She would be happy to have it back.

My fingers passed over the button on the top, and a tingling shock ran through me. Holding my breath, I pushed it. The petals fell open, just as they had for Jo. I couldn't breathe as I brought it up to my face, drinking in the paintings on each remaining petal.

They were truly amazing. The paintings were so detailed and bright that it was hard to believe they weren't real and moving. But they couldn't be of actual places, because in one there was the fiery mountain of Three O'Clock, and in another, Nine O'Clock, there was a woman standing in a blizzard and she was glowing bright white.

I don't know how long I sat staring at the pictures, rotating the watch slowly in my fingers so that I could see them all, before I heard something faint down the hall. It was a phone ringing. *Wes's phone.* I checked the time, my eyes wide: 11:02. *Who would call this late?*

I could hear Wes walk into the hall just outside my room, but he was whispering. I couldn't make out the words, and I wasn't brave enough to crack open the door and listen. A minute or two later I heard fast footsteps coming down the hall. I quickly threw the watch into a pocket of my pajama bottoms, shoving the chain in after it. I listened. Then the front door slammed.

I raced to the window that faced the driveway, watching the shadowy shape of Wes, an overcoat tossed over his T-shirt and sweatpants, as he rushed into his car.

I was breathing hard. I was afraid.

What the heck is going on? Did Jo call? Or the hospital? Or...

I tried to calm my nerves. It was probably something for work. But . . . it was so late.

After about a half hour I saw the flicker of headlights reappear from the driveway below. I tiptoed to the side of the window and peeked out.

I couldn't see my dad's face, but something about his walk as he headed back inside told me that he was far more tired than when he'd left, with his hunched shoulders and heavy steps. He slammed the front door again, then clomped up the stairs.

I shut out my light, hid underneath the covers, and pretended to be asleep, just in case he'd check in on me, but he only passed by my room. I heard his bedroom door click shut.

And everything was the same again. But I was tired now, the long day finally hitting me. The bed was comfortable, the sky was dark, and the watch I was now holding felt warm in my fist—like it was actually alive or something. The warmth calmed me, as if I were lying by the fireplace at Jo's house. I clicked it open and watched the long hands spin. I imagined Jo's hand scratching through my hair.

I stared at the waves painted on one of the petals. A wild ocean that filled my mind with gray.

Then I drifted off to sleep just as the minute hand reached 11:56.

ELEVEN

The bed rocked under me, and my skin prickled from the . . . cold?

Then something hit my nose, like a tapping or a dripping. Yeah, that was it. A drip, drip, drip . . .

The realization hit me: *It's rain.* I opened my eyes. My head was so filled with fog that I couldn't see clearly.

I looked down and realized I wasn't even in my bed. This wasn't my room. It was a *rock.* I was sitting on a giant rock, floating in the ocean. *This has to be a dream,* I thought. *Rocks don't float.*

"Holy moly," I muttered aloud.

I crab-walked backward, away from the edge. But as I moved, so did the rock, teetering with me, and I had to scramble to the middle to avoid falling over the edge. I'd never learned to swim, even in my dreams.

I glanced over the lip of the rock and saw the darkness of the water below.

Fog collected above the water, drifting up in spiraling tendrils, creating a blanket of gray that made it impossible to see my hands.

Then I noticed that every time a drop hit the surface of the ocean, it created a little hiss and a puff of steam.

"That doesn't even make sense," I whispered to myself as I huddled in the middle of the rock. "Why would rain make steam?"

And then I remembered.

Wasn't there supposed to be a sea in Eleven O'Clock that was so hot it would "burn the skin right off of you"? That had to be what was making the steam, because the rain was cool.

It had been so many years since I'd dreamed about Jo's stories. I tried slapping myself awake, but apparently, that only works in movies. I was trapped. Then I heard something.

It was a sort of crackling that shook down to my bones and made my skin itch. It sounded like electricity, and heat, and danger. Wes would say, *"You can't hear danger,"* but it's the only way I can explain it.

I turned to see what was making the noise, slowly,

my blood crawling icy through my veins, sweat prickling through my skin.

And there it was, a massive wall, planted in the middle of the water.

I froze at the sight of it.

It was so tall and was made of some kind of energy that shone many colors that swirled together. It crackled again.

My rock was floating toward it, and I was scared. I was going to crash into it.

As I got closer to the giant wall, I could see the energy swirling off it in clouds. It looked like glowing smoke, the wisps of which swirled around it. I breathed the swirling energy in. It burned my nose, and my throat, and my chest. My mind had gone fuzzy.

I tried to move, but my arms and legs were shaking so much that it was almost impossible.

I didn't understand what the wall was doing to me, but it was too hard to think. I just lay there, belly down now in the middle of the floating rock. I felt like I was drowning in the smoke.

Then I felt something heavy hit the ground beside me, rocking the island. I heard footsteps.

And then everything went dark and quiet.

. . .

I breathed in deeply, only kind of aware that I was coughing. I saw a clear glimpse of the sky above, not the white ceiling at Dad's house. I was still dreaming, then. I gasped as I rolled onto my side.

"What . . . is going—"

"So, you are alive." Someone was standing above me, but I couldn't see who it was beyond the brightness of the sun.

"What are you doing?" I asked.

"Way to be gracious. I helped you *breathe*. You got Smoke Sick."

I squinted up and finally saw her.

She was tall—taller than me, at least. She looked older, too, by a few years. She wore pants that ballooned at the legs and buckled at her calves, a frilled shirt, and a velvet coat with a pointy collar. Her shoes were colorful. She wore a glittering mask over her eyes and a belt slung low on her hips, outfitted with a variety of strange tools: a nail, a knife, a piece of white tile.

I looked away quickly, blushing. I had stared at her for too long.

"What's Smoke Sick?" I asked.

"Huh, she told me that you wouldn't know much, but I didn't realize that you wouldn't know *anything*. Geez, taking care of you is going to be like taking care of a baby."

I coughed again, ignoring her. *Even in my dreams people are jerks.*

"And no 'thanks' for saving your life even? Sheesh!"

"Thanks." *I guess.*

"That didn't even sound sincere! I was in the middle of something, you know. And just because Jo told me that some kid was coming who could save us, I decided to help you. But swimming out to the Wall on an Islet, wearing strange clothes? Why did I bother?"

My head swam, still filled with the smoke, I think. *Jo? Wall? Islet?* But my mouth formed words before I could stop it. "What do you mean my clothes are weird? Your clothes are weird."

I made the mistake of looking up at the girl again. I expected her to get mad, but she just laughed.

"You are a strange one, aren't you? You remind me of her."

I threw my arms up. Nothing she said made sense. I just wanted to get out of here. *Wake up,* I pleaded with myself. *Please just wake up.*

"Good thing she told us that you'd probably appear on the Mire. That's where she usually ended up. Without me waiting for you, you would have been a goner for sure."

I'd heard the word before: "mire." We'd learned about it in science. Mires were made of mud. "This isn't a mire," I said. "It's not made of mud."

Now she grinned, but it didn't look kind. It was the sort of smile that said she knew more than me.

"Technically correct, it isn't mud, but you're still wrong," she said, pulling a coil of tattered rope from her belt. "I didn't call it *a* mire, I called it *the* Mire. It's a fire marsh—"

"Fire marsh?" *There's no such thing*, I thought. I must be dreaming about Jo's clock world—Eleven O'Clock.

"Right. It's not mud or water," she continued. Then she uncoiled the rope. It fell, bouncing once, before hitting the surface of the ocean—but it wasn't an ocean at all. As the tip of the rope sank below the fog, it connected with the pool only to light on fire as soon as it did. The girl grimaced, dropping it. The rest of the rope sank, turning to black dust.

I huddled in the middle of the rock again, where it felt safe. I didn't know if you could die in a dream, but I didn't want to test it.

"If Jo really did send you, then you must be strong." She leaned in closer to me, and I backed away. "But you don't *look* strong."

I sighed to myself. This had gone on long enough.

I wasn't going to be insulted by a girl who wasn't even real.

"This is just a dream," I mumbled to myself, crossing my arms.

She glanced back at me with an eyebrow raised. "A . . . dream?"

I nodded, waving my hands through the air. "All a dream."

She shook her head. "She said you might say strange things like that."

"And you're just a frilly dream pirate."

Her face was still blank. I flinched as she suddenly crouched down by me. "I don't know why you're supposed to be so special, but no matter who you are, you ought to be more careful. You never know who you're talking to." She sounded so serious. It made me a bit scared, but I found I could neither speak nor look away.

Then she flicked me in the nose.

"Hey!"

But instead of saying anything more, she stood up. I looked around, rubbing my nose, and realized that I could no longer hear the crackle of the Wall.

"Where are we?" I asked.

"Heading back," she said without looking at me. She

stood on the edge of the Islet, leaning on it with her toes like it was a skateboard.

"Back where?"

"Home—or Eleven, as Jo calls it."

My head began to throb. *Just like I thought.*

The throb in my head ran down my arms. I finally noticed the round thing clenched in my fist. *The watch!* It was still warm. I opened my hand to look at it and gasped.

Instead of the gold pocket watch, it had become an orb of multicolored energy. It was still shaped like a clock, but it glowed and flashed, like electricity . . . *Like the Wall,* I realized. I held it to my ear and listened to it hum.

"Where did you get that?"

I looked up at the girl. She was staring at the ball of energy that was once my watch with a bold fascination, like the nurse had. I wouldn't let her have it, not even in a dream.

I closed the ball back in my fist, away from her gaze.

"It's mine" was all I could think to say.

She strode to me, causing the Islet to slow down.

"Let me see it again."

"No." I shoved the ball of energy into my pocket.

She stared at me, and I stared right back. I could tell

she was debating something, the way her eyes flicked over my pocket, to my hand, to my face, but she resigned herself to step back. "Fine. Maybe I shouldn't have come all the way out here to save you, after all."

"Why *did* you come?"

"Jo told us to."

"Right, but *why*?"

She turned back to me, frowning. "Because she said you would help us."

"Help you do what?"

"Destroy the Wall."

I snorted. "As if I even care."

A second later I was flat on my back. The heel of her shoe had struck me in the chest.

"I told you to be careful about what you say."

"Ow! Geez! What was that for?"

"That Wall divides us from the other hours. It means that I, *we*, don't have any freedom—not like *you*. You can leave whenever you want. We are trapped here."

"Why don't you just, I don't know, fly over it or something?"

She rolled her eyes, turning back to the edge, guiding the Islet once more. "She told us that you would help, but clearly, you don't know the first thing about anything."

"Yeah, well, Jo has said a lot of things."

"What do you mean by that?" She shot me a sharp look.

"Nothing, it's just, well, she's sick. She doesn't know what she's saying."

"You're lying. She never told us she was sick."

Something about the way she said it made me angry, and my face grew hot. "Well, if she wasn't sick, would she have given me this?" I asked, holding up the ball of energy again for a second before stuffing it back away.

The girl's eyes were wide.

"It's not possible, but . . . if Jo gave you the Smoke Ball, then that would mean she couldn't come see us—"

I shrieked, distracted by a bug that nearly hit me in the forehead.

It was long, like a caterpillar, and skinny, like a piece of string—so thin that its body wobbled as it flew. It had many fat little legs dangling from its body and two large black wings that shot from the sides, folding up and down as it hobbled through the air.

"What is that?"

Then the bug zoomed straight for the deadly surface of the Mire.

I looked up at the girl, who didn't seem worried at all. "That's a Mirefly. You might want to duck, by the way."

"Why?" But seconds later I knew.

The long fly pierced back up through the ocean. Its body had been lit and was entirely *on fire*, like the wick of a candle. Its long wings looked shorter and more powerful as they beat through the flames, up into the air.

The fly shot over my head. I ducked just barely in time and still smelled the sizzle of my flyaway hairs. I patted them down.

"So, you don't know what a Mirefly is, or the Mire for that matter, or an Islet, or the Wall, or Eleven," the girl sneered. "But you're supposed to save us and you have your own Smoke Ball."

"It's not a Smoke Ball. It's a watch."

"Well, it looks like it's made of smoke, and that's what Jo called it. She said it allowed her spirit to enter our world, right?"

I refused to answer anymore. I was sick of her already. I just shrugged my shoulders instead.

"I think soon you will become either my favorite or my least favorite person in all of Eleven," she said.

It was a strange admission that made my cheeks feel hot.

"What's your name?" she asked.

I considered lying, but what could it hurt? We were in a dream, after all.

"I'm Rose."

"That's an awfully bad name. You're not rosy at all! I'm Fleck." As she said it, she smiled. The freckles on her cheeks shone brightly under the sun. "Well, not-so-rosy Rose, it appears we're here."

"Where?"

I glanced around her and saw it. We were headed for a much larger island ahead, an island with a city on it. A circle of clouds hovered above it, the city casting ghostly colors on the bottoms of the clouds. From a distance it was hard to see the people on the island, but it was colorful, loud, and full of movement.

It looked like a party.

Then Fleck stepped in front of me, blocking my view. "Is that Eleven?"

She slipped a piece of tile and the nail off her belt. Then she began carving something into it. "Sure is. I don't think we should travel there together, though. Wouldn't want anyone to catch us. So we'll split up and meet on land. Jo told you where to go, right? To the cemetery?"

"Wait, what? How are you going to get to shore? Are you planning to swim through *fire*?"

She glanced over at me with a half smile. "You're not the only powerful one here." She then looked back down at her tile and finished a few lines.

Seconds later the center of the tile glowed a light purple. Fleck held it out from her body, watching as a large, gleaming shape poured from it, growing bigger and bigger. I backed away as the shape formed into a small, delicately carved sailboat that bobbed on the Mire. She stepped onto it. The glow subsided, revealing that the boat was made of the same smooth stone as the tile.

"Okay, that's pretty cool."

She looked almost surprised before she smiled. "Thanks. See you there!" She handled the sails, directing them away from my Islet.

"Rosemary."

I heard a faint voice that seemed to drift down from above me.

"Rosemary."

It was growing stronger, closer. It sounded like it was coming from the city. I turned to look toward it. The colors in the clouds pulsated as the voice grew louder.

"Rosemary!"

THE BAD NEWS

Rosemary! Wake up."

My eyes burst open. I was hot and sweating. The warmth seemed to come from something squeezed tightly in my fist. *The watch!*

I was lying, curled, on something soft. *It's my bed,* I realized, disappointed and relieved at the same time. *So it was only a dream.*

I heard Wes's voice. "Rosemary! Can you hear me?"

I hurried to the door, my heart thumping.

I ripped the door open to see Wes on the other side. He had deep circles under his eyes. He was already dressed in a crisp suit, however, his hair slicked back.

"What is it?"

He thrust my backpack toward me.

"Why?"

"Time for us to go," he said. He turned and trod with heavy feet down the hall. "Put on your clothes. Meet me in the car."

I glanced at the clock on the wall. It was just before 8:00 a.m.

"Wait, I—"

But he was already gone.

My brain was fuzzy from the dream, and I couldn't quite grasp what was happening. I coughed. My lungs still felt like they were filled with smoke or whatever. *That's weird*, I thought as I rushed to brush my teeth and toss my dirty clothes on.

I threw my stuff into my bag, coming at last to the gold watch. I lifted it carefully.

Can I really keep it? Jo had given it to me. But she had obviously been really sick when she did, and she had said it was the most important thing she owned. I imagined when she got better again, she would want it back. *I should take it to her, just in case.* I would ask Wes to take me back to the hospital today so I could visit her again. Maybe she was feeling better already.

Wes was waiting in the car, his gaze straight ahead. He looked mad, but what had I done? I hopped into the passenger seat. I was too scared to say anything as he pulled the car out of the driveway.

"What happened in the hospital?" he asked, his voice quiet.

"Huh?"

"What did she say to you?"

"Uh, I told you already. It was just some weird stuff about magic that I didn't really understand."

He sucked air in between his teeth, hissing. I could tell he was annoyed but was trying to hold it in. "No, what *else* did she say?"

I felt my heart speeding up. *He doesn't know about the watch, does he?*

"Nothing really, we just talked about art and stuff."

He nodded, refusing to look at me. After a long silence I dared to speak. "Actually, I was wondering if I could go back to visit her today and—"

"She's gone."

"What?"

"She ran away from the hospital last night. No one knows where she went." He paused, then continued, "Do *you* have any idea where she would go?"

I shook my head. My throat felt like it was closing up. Besides the fantasy world, Jo never talked about wanting to go anywhere.

I hoped that this was just one of her pranks or something, that she was really fine out there somewhere, but worries nibbled at my stomach. *What if she's not okay?* Yesterday she had been really, really sick. Maybe she *did* need to be in the hospital.

"Are you taking me home or to Mom's work?"

"Neither, I'm taking you to school."

"But I thought you already called in my absence for today."

"That was before Jo disappeared. Now I have to deal with it, and your mother is at work. Just"—he waved his hand in the air, never looking at me—"explain it to your teacher. I'm sure he'll understand."

"But I didn't do my homework, and my phone's dead, and I didn't shower, and I'm wearing the same clothes as—"

He finally looked at me. I immediately shut up. He seemed really tired.

"Come on, Rosemary. It's fine. It's one day. Can you do this for me?"

"Yeah," I whispered.

We didn't talk the rest of the drive.

The air inside the car was thick, and Wes's mug of coffee, steaming in the cup holder in front of me, smelled stronger than usual. It was like the car had to be filled with something else when it wasn't filled with talking. But even if I'd wanted to speak, I couldn't. I was too focused on one thought and the many possibilities that surrounded it:

What happened to Jo?

THE NEW KID

By the time we reached school, the bell was about to ring and students and teachers alike were rushing all over, like a swarm of bees.

Wes dropped me off out front. I had no intention of going to class—but he waited in the lot watching, so I had to hide in the hallway. Sneaking out without anyone noticing was going to be hard.

The halls of the school were crowded. Too crowded, and everyone was screaming and running. *I just have to get outside and then I can escape.*

"Hey! Grossy Rosey!"

Ugh. Jeremiah.

"Don't ignore me, Grossy!"

Maybe I could lose him in the crowd. The faster I walked, the closer his voice sounded. I refused to stop.

"Grossy!" He snatched the loop on the top of my backpack. "Why are you running?"

Jeremiah stared down at me with a big smile on his face. Teachers thought Jeremiah was a good kid because he was always smiling.

"Leave me alone." I yanked against him. He held me harder, so I pulled again. He let go of my backpack at the worst second, and I tumbled forward, falling on my knees.

Kids stopped for a second to point and whisper at me. I could feel the blush taking over my cheeks.

"Oops! You shouldn't have pulled so hard. I didn't mean to do that."

Yes, you did.

It was like I could feel the blood racing through my veins. Mom said that's called "adrenaline." Sometimes when I had too much adrenaline, I just cried. I really didn't want to cry in front of Jeremiah.

"Let me help you." He held a hand out to me as if he were really trying to be helpful.

I knew better. He would probably pull me up really hard and make my arm hurt, or he'd let go at the last second and I'd fall again. He'd pretend it was an accident.

Instead, I pushed myself up, refusing to look at him.

"Why are you ignoring me, Rosey? I just want to ask you about the homework—wait, are you wearing the same clothes as yesterday?"

Of course he'd notice. He always paid attention, it seemed like, just so he could find the tiniest things about me to make fun of.

I'm not sure what I did to make him hate me. I felt like the only reason he picked on me was because I didn't have any friends who could help me fight back. *Well, if my only choices are people like Jeremiah, then maybe I don't want to have friends.*

"You don't even change your clothes! Ew, you really *are* Grossy Rosey."

I don't know if it was because I was too tired from my weird dreams and worrying about Jo, but I got angry, and my stomach was hot, and for once I didn't want to ignore it. I turned around to face him.

"Why do you even *know* what I was wearing yesterday, Jeremiah?"

His smile dropped.

"I don't pay attention to *you*," I continued, my voice quivering, "so why do you pay attention to *me*?"

A couple of people had stopped to look at us. I could feel my adrenaline rising. I really, really didn't want to cry, but I felt like I had already gone so far that I couldn't run away now.

"I don't pay attention to you!" he spat at me. "You're just so gross, it's hard to ignore you."

"Then try harder." I glared at him before spinning around on my heels. A tiny voice in the back of my head reminded me that it was his birthday today. Then, with a clench in my gut, I realized, *And Fallon's*. This would be the first year since kindergarten that I wasn't invited to her party.

Maybe I shouldn't have been so mean to Jeremiah today of all days.

Of course, he changed my mind.

"Wait! No! Where are you going? You can't just say that and then—"

I felt him snatch the back of my backpack again. I'd probably embarrassed him. That wasn't smart of me. People do mean things sometimes when they're embarrassed.

"Jer!"

Both our heads turned. It was Fallon. Her long blond hair was tied up in two braids.

"What are you doing? We're going to be late to class."

She looked at him the whole time, never even

acknowledging me. I wondered, maybe if I started dressing more like the popular girls and learned to braid my hair like she did . . . would she like me again?

Would it be worth it?

"You go, I'm busy," he said to his sister. I felt Jeremiah shake my backpack a bit, sending rumbles all the way through my arms and legs.

"Whatever, Jer, let's—"

"Hey, what's up?"

It was the new boy, Alejandro. He was wearing high-tops and a yellow leather jacket. I'd never seen someone wear a yellow leather jacket before. It was kind of cool.

"We're talking," Jeremiah snapped.

Alejandro raised just one eyebrow at him. "Then why are you holding her backpack?"

"She fell down!" he sputtered back, letting go of me.

"Jeremiah!" Fallon pulled on her brother's hand. "We're going to be late."

As Jeremiah let her drag him to class, he pointed at us. "Why don't they have to come?"

"Oh, I'm very sick right now. I have to go to the nurse before I puke on you," Alejandro said.

Jeremiah then looked at me.

"Uh, me too," I stammered. "I'm going to puke on you too"—it was all I could think to say.

Before Jeremiah could ask any more questions, Fallon pulled him into the crowd. I could just hear him shout, "Why is she so weird?" before they disappeared.

But class was almost starting. Now I didn't have much time to escape.

"Thanks!" I called over my shoulder to Alejandro before I raced down the hallway, the exit door in sight.

It wasn't until I was outside that I heard footsteps behind me. I spun around.

It was Alejandro.

"Where are you going now?" he asked.

"Didn't you just say you were sick?"

"Oh, that." He laughed. "I made that up so that guy would leave us alone."

Leave us *alone?*

"Then aren't you going to get in trouble for ditching?"

Alejandro shrugged. "Aren't you?"

I didn't have an answer for that, and I didn't want to think about it, so I just kept walking.

Our campus used to be a Catholic school, and there's an old church in the back that no one likes to go into anymore. Everybody says it's haunted.

I love it.

Sure, it's kind of dirty and cold, but it almost feels

magical. Like it's an old castle or something. It's filled with dark but colorful paintings.

I discovered the church earlier this year when I had no friends to eat lunch with.

In the church I could paint and look at paintings and hide in the dark corners. Nobody ever found me in there, and I had never shown it to anyone either.

So why did I take the new kid there?

Mostly because I had nowhere else to go and he insisted on following me.

"This," I said, spinning in the middle of the big stone floor, "is the haunted *church*." I said the last word loudly so that it would echo up the tall roof. I heard the tapping of Alejandro's feet as he approached.

"What's it haunted with?"

We both looked up one long wall, old painted faces staring back. The windows were made of colored glass that shone rainbows on the gray bricks inside.

"I don't know," I responded, looking at him. "Ghosts, probably?"

He looked back at me. "Neat."

"Yeah, neat."

"Ooh, what's that?" he asked, walking toward the opposite corner.

"Wait, stop—"

He was walking to the biggest window. Underneath was my easel. Stacked high next to the easel were all of the paintings I'd been working on during lunch.

"Don't touch those."

But it was too late. He stood in front of the one I'd been working on yesterday at lunch, right before Dad came.

It was an oil painting of a big ship that Aunt Jo had told me about once. She said that it looked like a castle, but it floated above the water, carried by many flying caterpillars with black wings. They were tied by long strings to the castle.

Now that I looked at the bugs again, they reminded me strangely of the Mireflies.

Huh, maybe I dreamed about them because I had been painting them. That made sense.

I had thought the floating castle was a beautiful thing when she had told me about it, but I realized I'd never see it unless I painted it, so I did. A lot of my paintings are things Jo told me about that I wanted to see.

I had been working on it for a week, coming back day after day. It was almost finished. I *would* work on it at home, but Wes thought it was a useless hobby and Mom was always worried that I would get paint on the furniture.

"Who made this?"

Alejandro had already reached out before I could stop him. He trailed his hand across a lantern on the castle ship. An orange line from a big glob of undried oil paint followed his finger all the way up to one of the Mireflies.

"Oops! I didn't mean to mess it up, I didn't realize it was wet." He reached out again to try to rub the line out, but I snatched his hand in the middle of the air. "I'm so unlucky."

"It's fine."

"But whoever painted it might get mad."

"No, they won't," I said as I grabbed a brush from the table by the easel and started touching up the smear.

"How do you know?" he asked.

"Because *I* painted it."

"Wait, really?"

I winced at his shock. Very few people had ever seen my paintings before.

"It's the best thing I've ever seen!" he said, leaning in to take a closer look.

"You . . . you think so?"

"Well, not the *best* thing—the best thing I've ever seen is a mac 'n' cheese pizza—but it's a really good thing."

I smiled. That wasn't the *best* thing someone could say, but it *was* a really good thing.

"Oh, shoot, and I messed it up! I'm sorry. How can I help you fix it?"

"It's fine." I looked at the orange streak. "I like it, actually. Looks like a fireball or something." *More like a skid mark, but who cares? No one else is ever going to see it anyway.*

"I don't even know how you learn to do something like that."

"I just practice a lot is all."

"You know what it reminds me of?"

"What?"

"*Torch Throwers.*" His face lit up as he sat on the ground, pulling his tablet out of his backpack. "Let me show you."

Alejandro clicked the tablet on. The screen was covered in bright game icons.

"Which one is *Torch Throwers*?" I asked.

"This one. It's just a tapping game, but the art's cool." He almost sounded embarrassed as he said it, looking up at me with unsure eyes.

I knew that tone of voice. My voice sounded like it all the time. "I like cool art."

He smiled back, sliding half of the tablet into my

hands. "You play offense, then. I'll play defense."

As soon as he touched the icon with a flaming torch on it, tinkling music played. The screen burst bright with colors. Front and center was a castle—it was white and gold and looked as if it were painted right onto the tablet itself. A bright red START appeared in the middle of the castle.

"Ready?"

He tapped it. The music became fast and loud, and the colors grew brighter—more alive. Little people ran out from the side and stood in front of the big wooden drawbridge. On my side of the screen they carried torches. On the right side they carried shields.

"Get ready for it," he said.

Then, from behind the castle, a giant shape emerged from the shadows. It was dark and scaly and angry.

A dragon.

Its big wings wrapped around the castle, nearly cracking it in two. Its eyes gleamed red as it shrieked into the orange sky.

"All right, tap."

I did. One of the little people threw their torch. It hit the dragon, and the dragon growled.

"Okay, my turn."

The dragon spat flames at us. Alejandro tapped his screen, and one of the shielded people jumped forward, blocking the fireball from hitting the townspeople.

"So we have to stop the dragon?" I asked.

"We have to stop the dragon."

"Easy."

It wasn't.

As we kept playing, our little people started disappearing—wiped out by the dragon's wings as it swiped at them or burned away by fireballs.

But we kept tapping, Alejandro's shouts growing louder. Together it seemed like we might actually win. I couldn't imagine playing this game alone.

Finally, the dragon began to wobble. There were only two little people left, however—one shield holder and one torch thrower. Alejandro and I were screaming at each other.

"TAP NOW!"

"TAP! TAP! TAP!"

The last tiny woman on the right leaped forward with her shield while the tiny man on the left threw his last torch.

The dragon exhaled a final burst of flames that took over the whole screen, burning bright.

"TAP!" I screamed.

But it was too late. All the shields and torches were gone.

When the light from the explosion cleared, nothing was left but the castle in ruins. The walls were filled with holes, and the roof had fallen down.

YOU LOSE danced across the screen.

Alejandro and I sat in silence. Then I spoke. "Well, that was . . ."

"Kind of depressing?" Alejandro finished for me.

"Kind of," I said.

"Yeah, I'm not sure how to beat it, honestly. I thought maybe together we could."

"To-together?"

"Sure," he answered, beaming. "Why not?"

After last summer it seemed like no one wanted to do anything with me. Now even Jo was gone, right when I thought I'd gotten her back. I stared down at Alejandro's tablet.

Then the castle rebuilt itself, the sun reappeared in the sky, and everything went back to the way it was at the beginning. START appeared again in big bright letters.

"I wish I could do that in real life," I whispered to myself.

"Do what in real life?"

"Just undo everything and start over."

He looked at me but didn't say anything. It wasn't a mean silence, though, or a confused silence. It was just like he was thinking.

I had only known Alejandro for, what, an hour? And already I felt more comfortable with him than any of the other kids in school.

"I think my parents tried to do that when we moved back here," he said finally.

"Where are you from?"

"I'm not from anywhere. That's the problem. My parents just keep pressing the restart button." I looked at him, confused. He continued, "We started here, see? I was actually born in Arizona. But, uh"—he looked down with a sigh—"some bad stuff happened. An accident. And we had to move to live with Dad's family in Mexico City." I wanted to ask him about it, but I sensed he didn't want to say any more as he rolled on. "Then Mom got a job in California, then Houston, then Florida. It sucks because I never got to actually feel comfortable anywhere, you know?"

Wow, he's lived in more places than I've even been to.

"Why did you move so much?"

"Bad things just kept happening. Accidents. Mistakes.

I don't know why. It was like every time things just started to get good, something terrible would pop up and we'd have to leave again."

"I'm sorry," I said, not sure what else *to* say.

He shrugged. "It's fine. The thing I've realized is that you just have to find a way to make yourself happy wherever you are." His dark expression turned bright as he looked up at me and smiled. "Whenever something bad happens, something good will follow. So you shouldn't restart your game. Just keep playing and wait for the good thing. Yeah?"

"I guess . . . but what's the good thing about losing *Torch Throwers* and all the little people getting burned up?"

"That we get to play it again."

I nodded, thinking about everything he'd said. I couldn't ignore the question nibbling at my belly, though, some of which I said out loud and some of which I kept to myself: "Why did you stand up for me"—*and follow me here, and play a game with me, and now want to play* again *with me*—"and stuff?"

Alejandro lay back on the stone floor, spreading out his arms and legs like a starfish. "I've gone to a lot of schools, and I've met a lot of people, and most of them didn't like me."

"Why not?"

Alejandro shrugged, still lying on his back. "I think it's because I was always new, which meant I was always different, and the more different I felt, the quieter I was. The quieter I was, the meaner people became."

A shiver ran up my spine. I knew exactly what he meant.

"But now that I'm back here, I want a fresh start! I'm going to trust my gut—even if it gets me in trouble sometimes—and my gut said that you were someone who needed help."

"I thought you said your gut was going to puke." Now I lay back too.

"Yeah, sure, maybe both."

We laughed, the giggles echoing up the stone walls.

Then there was a short silence. I heard Alejandro's leather jacket scraping against the ground as he sat up.

"Who was that guy, anyway?"

"Oh, Jeremiah?" I groaned. "I used to be friends with his sister, but then it was like everyone just . . . changed, and I didn't. They started dressing cooler, hanging out in little groups, texting inside jokes that I didn't know. I just didn't get it, like I'm an alien or something." I looked up at him from the floor, upside down. "They stopped wanting to hang out with me.

Then they started getting mean. It became cool to *be* mean to me, you know?"

He nodded.

"Whatever. It doesn't matter, I guess. I don't need friends." The second I said it, I almost regretted it. Like I was insulting Alejandro.

"Where do you eat lunch?"

"Usually here by myself. Why?"

"Well, maybe I could join you sometime. I have a lot more games I could show you."

I abruptly sat up and my eyes widened. "Wait, really?" I hadn't meant to say it.

"I mean, if you want me to."

"Sure!" I said too quickly. "That could be cool."

"Cool," he repeated, then he stood up and threw his stuff back into his bag. "I should probably get to class now before I *really* get in trouble."

As he took the stone steps that led to the door, I wrestled with a thought—something I wanted to say but was embarrassed to.

"Hey, Alejandro?" He turned to look back at me. "Thanks."

He smiled and nodded before closing the door behind him.

After Alejandro left, I didn't want to follow. I just

really didn't feel like facing everyone else. So I painted instead.

I picked up the brush and worked on the castle picture, painting little fireball lines with a smile, thinking of Alejandro's face when he'd messed it up.

And when I finished that canvas, I moved on to a blank one.

I started blobbing out the shapes of a large stone floating in the middle of a fiery marsh and the figure of a tall, frilly pirate girl.

I remembered her face in every detail, down to the freckle.

Then I started in on a new picture of that monster I'd dreamed about in class yesterday.

I painted until my fingers became stiff, then I sighed, lying down on one of the pews. How long had it been now? What was I going to do for the rest of the day? I couldn't paint anymore, and I would have to wait here until Mom was done with work at 3:00. Then I could call and have her pick me up.

I pulled the watch out of my pocket and popped it open. It was just past 11:00.

I watched the hands spin, and my eyes suddenly grew heavy. It was like the night before. Just looking at the watch made me feel so—I yawned—*sleepy*.

I'm not sure how long it took me to fall asleep. I imagined the dark Mire from the night before, how it had looked, how warm it had been, and how close we had been to the land. I wanted to know what it looked like in that magical place.

The visions blurred into black.

ELEVEN

*B*oom. *Scratch.*

The ground shook. It felt familiar somehow, but strange. My eyes cracked open. I winced at the light—and then the ground moved again.

Boom. Scratch.

My eyes shot wide.

I was in the dreamworld again. Everything looked the same as the night before, except my Islet had left the Mire and was now *climbing* back onto land.

Afraid of falling, I scrambled to the edge. I peered over the gray lip of it and saw a field of black sand below.

Then I saw the leg. Thick and trunklike, covered in black scales that gleamed blue in the light. The leg raised up from beneath the Islet and stomped onto the sand.

Boom.

It pulled the Islet forward, across the sand and shells and rocks.

Scra-atch.

I nearly rolled off as it pulled itself forward.

Boom. Scratch.

It eased its way out of the Mire, the tide of which I could see shimmering and rippling on the bank behind me.

Thump.

I lost sense of myself as the Islet seemed to walk upward. I watched, too scared to look down. We were heading toward a pile of boulders beneath a big cliff.

Thump. Thump. Thump.

I heard a huff from beneath me that reverberated throughout the Islet. A moment later the Islet dropped to the ground.

Afraid of what it might do next, I slid off the back, collapsing onto the sand below.

Could it be real? Was Jo telling the truth about the watch? I felt a tiny bit of hope, but I imagined Wes scoffing in my head. *"Magic isn't real,"* he'd say. All the kids at school would laugh at me if they thought I believed in magic, and yet this was like no dream I had ever had before.

I turned around to look back at the Islet. It had a large, flat shell that was weathered and stony, lumps and bumps all over. Four fat legs curled underneath it. The tail was long and whipped from side to side. I trembled as I finally looked up at its head.

One spiraling orange eye peeked out from under thick, horned brows.

I was unable to look away as two pointed ears unfurled, swiveling toward me. I backed away slowly but tripped on a rock and stumbled with a yelp.

As if they were robots, the heads of all the Islets surrounding me rose, orange eyes stared, and ears unfurled and pointed directly at me.

I ran.

It was another few moments before I heard the screaming—shrill and high, terrified. And a few moments more until I realized that *I* was the one screaming.

As I darted between boulders, I was vaguely aware that they were rising around me. Standing. Moving. They were slow but massive, and I had to move twice as fast as I ever had before to avoid getting stomped.

I didn't pay attention to where the Islets were going, but I could feel the ground shaking as their thick feet pounded against it. I could hear the booms of their cries as they jabbered to one another in a clicking, roaring language that sounded part turtle, part dinosaur.

I continued to run, over the sand, across the beach, and then up. I scrabbled along the cliff, like a rat, until I reached a set of stairs carved into the stone.

Now that I felt safe, I finally looked down, my chest puffing.

Uh-oh.

The Islets were all running now, in the opposite direction I had been. I could feel them, making the earth shake and landslides fall.

I'd caused a stampede.

"Oops."

"I've been looking all over for you."

I heard the whisper before I saw her. Then I felt a yank on my arm, and I finally tore my eyes away from the chaos below. I looked up to see the girl from last night, Fleck.

"Why didn't you go to the cemetery like I told you? And now *this*? You really do know nothing."

Before I could speak, she tugged me up the rock stairs.

"Come on. We have to get out before he finds you."

"Who?"

"Just *move*." She pulled harder.

"Whoa, wait! Who—" But I couldn't even finish,

because she pulled so hard and the stairs were so uneven that I had to focus just to not fall off the cliff.

We soon reached the top, and I got my first glance of the city.

It was massive and loud and vibrant. The buildings looked normal, but they were every different color you could imagine and more—stacked up on one another so high, you couldn't see the tops of them.

Just in front of us was a stack that began with a blue house, and then, right there on its shingled roof was a second house, a salmon-pink one precariously balanced, and above that a brick house covered in fairy lights. Some didn't seem to be balanced right, and others were at funny angles.

Through the windows I could see the things going on inside: dancing and fighting and wildness. They looked like dollhouses.

As Fleck pulled me, we entered the city, and I could hear the sounds of drums and trumpets. The whole city was filled with music—so loud that I could feel the low bass line rumble through my feet and up my legs, wobbling them.

"Is it a party or something?"

Fleck finally stopped for a moment and turned

around to look at me with a funny expression like she couldn't quite believe what I'd said.

"It's always a party at Eleven." She then pulled a mask down over her face—glittering silver with swirling black lines—that covered her eyes and nose. "Put yours on."

"I don't have a mask," I said.

She sighed and tore off a bit of the frill around her neck and then pulled a pen from her belt. She drew a mask shape on the frill. As she drew the lines, they glowed a faint purple, like the tile had the night before.

Just as soon as she'd finished, light pooled around the shape and floated out—growing into a life-sized mask in front of her. The glowing mask then became the same white as the frill, with the same delicate, lacy pattern, especially around the eyeholes. It began to fall. Fleck snatched it out of the air.

"Here." She handed it to me along with a thin cord that she had pulled from her shirt's neckline.

I stared at the flimsy thing.

"Well, tie it on! We've got places to be, and that spell won't last forever."

"We've got places to be?" was all I could think to say as my shaking fingers, overwhelmed by everything that had already happened, tied the cord around the mask and slipped it on my face.

Fleck appraised me before nodding. "You may still be wearing funny clothes, but at least no one can tell who you are. Now hurry!"

She ran forward, and after a second of consideration I tagged along. She might not have been pulling me anymore, but I knew that I was still meant to follow.

We wound through crowds of people in the street. They were all masked. One man had a red mask with a long nose. Another wore a mask that covered her whole face, round like the moon. People wore wigs and frills and costumes, like Fleck.

The deeper we were pulled into the revelry of the city, the stranger people became, their screaming fouler, their movements wilder, and the music ever louder until I could feel it shaking even the tiniest bones in my ears.

"Where are we going?" I shouted to Fleck—not that the answer would have mattered much. I just didn't want to be *here* anymore. The walls of people were closing in. It made me anxious.

Fleck said something without turning around, but her words were lost in the chaos.

"What?" I screamed.

Her head turned, but she never stopped running. "The graveyard, I said—"

"Wait!" I shouted, but it was too late. She had plowed unseeingly into a tall man with a yellow velvet coat and a tall top hat.

"Good evening, children."

Fleck's face paled as she looked up at him.

He was taller than anyone I had ever seen in real life. His arms and legs were bone thin, and I could see the round outlines of his knees through his pants.

I knew who he was instantly, and I felt all of my veins grow cold. I was frozen.

The Smoke Keeper of Eleven.

"C-come on," Fleck whispered to me, but she couldn't seem to move either.

The man smiled down at her. His teeth were long, yellow, and cracked—but not as long as in Jo's drawings. He had almost no lips, and his large nose was broken in the center. I couldn't see his eyes beyond his mask. That frightened me, because I suspected, like Jo had said, that they weren't there at all. "Why are you in a rush? Where did you come from, little ones?"

The man looked past Fleck and straight at me. "I don't think I've seen you before"—his thin lips curled into a smile—"and I see everyone."

He stepped toward me, past Fleck. Her eyes were big and worried as she stared on.

The Smoke Keeper loomed over me, his very presence seeming to quiet the music and the party that surrounded us.

"What is your name and why are you a stranger to me?" The puff of his breath smelled horrible and made my stomach hurt. "Strangers get sent into the Wall, you know. Strangers don't belong here."

Help, I wanted to say to Fleck, but the word wouldn't leave my throat.

He was going to devour me, and I couldn't run.

The Smoke Keeper reached a hand out to me, trying to snatch up my wrist. I jerked away, but his long, curling fingernail sliced into my hand, making a C shape on the meat of my palm.

I winced. The pain was enough to shake me out of my fear. Then Fleck's warm hand slipped into mine, and she yanked me into the dancing crowd.

The townspeople linked arms, spun, and mashed their bodies together.

Over the heads of the dancers I could see the bobbing hat of the Smoke Keeper. Fleck tugged my hand harder, dragging me farther in until I couldn't see him anymore.

Then a tall woman wrapped her elbow around mine and spun me in a fast circle, breaking my connection with Fleck. The woman laughed at whatever ridiculous expression I had made, then set me loose—whirling and alone.

The walls of people began closing in again until all I could see was a blur. People spinning. Explosions. Drums.

I was flung around, my head whipping from side to side, searching for Fleck.

It's just a dream.

But then I saw the Smoke Keeper. He was coming right for me.

It's just a dream!

"Rose!"

Before I could process everything that was happening, Fleck was pulling me forward. We ran. Fast. Cutting corners, jumping walls, not looking back until we were racing across black sand. Another beach. There was an island just ahead. In the middle of the island was a tall building stack—but this one was entirely white. It looked like it was made of marble, and it reached up so high into the sky that I couldn't see the top.

"What is that?" I asked, panting, my hands on my knees.

"The graveyard."

Fleck made another boat out of tile. We sailed aboard

it to the island. On the other side the boat exploded into purple smoke.

I looked around. We were alone. I heaved a sigh when I realized the Smoke Keeper must not be following us anymore.

As we approached the white building, the ground was growing warmer and warmer, making my forehead sweat.

"Why is it so hot?"

She gave me a look that said I wasn't very smart. "Because it's a graveyard?"

All around the white building was a wide stretch of dirt and sand scattered with tombstones. From a distance it seemed that there were waves of green clouds moving across the surface of the ground, as if it were a murky swamp.

We approached the door of the white building, but the opening was so small that we had to crawl through.

Once inside, however, I was shocked to see how massive it was. The marble box was filled with tiny stone buildings with names written above the front doors. The stone buildings sat side by side, like a neighborhood.

But, you know, a neighborhood where everyone was dead.

I stared at a particularly pretty grave house—gray with gold veins threaded throughout the marble—and I felt more heat creep up from my shoes.

I followed after Fleck, who was already all the way down a corridor and turning out of sight.

She didn't say anything as she led me down long hallways of dead neighborhoods where the tombs became bigger. We were headed upward, it seemed, into the stacked tower of white buildings.

The farther we went, the darker it became. I ran my hands along the walls to keep my place, but I shuddered back when my hand ran across something that felt very different than the cool marble. I squinted at it.

"Bones?"

I heard Fleck sigh ahead, and I followed the sound.

"We're in the catacombs now. It's like a maze, so stay close behind."

"B-but why are there bones in the walls?"

She looked back at me, surprised. I could barely make out her face in the darkness. "Oh. There aren't bones *in* the walls." I sighed with relief. Then she continued, "The walls are *made* of bones."

A shiver ran through me as I looked again at the wall. A row of skulls stared back. *What a horrible place,* I thought, running to keep up with her.

We finally reached a row where the boxes had no doors sealing their fronts. These were unused graves. I peeked into one, lit from the inside by a fiery glow. I looked up, following the source of the glow to see a bird made of fire circling overhead, lighting the room from within.

"Whoa—ahh!" My surprise turned to fear when I looked down and saw a boy's big pink face.

Fleck finally turned around. "Oh, Jonquil, I found her. This is the girl Jo sent."

The boy climbed out. He was about a head taller than me and much, much wider. He reminded me of a brick, tall and squared off. His skin was sunburned to a nice pink. His hair was yellow. Not even blond, exactly, just yellow. Or maybe it *looked* more yellow against his pink face. I figured he was probably a year or two older than me.

"Where did you find her?"

Fleck shot me an angry look before climbing into the large, open tomb. "Back on the beach. What she was doing there for hours, I can't even imagine."

I climbed in after them. The tomb inside was almost . . . homey (if you could ever call a giant dead-people box made of bones "homey").

It was covered in pillows, cushions, and blankets. They were many colors, and it reminded me of a ball pit.

I waded through the cushions after Fleck and Jonquil, sitting on a big one that looked like a purple marshmallow.

When I looked up, three faces were staring at me.

I held in my surprise as I counted them.

Fleck.

Jonquil.

And now a smaller child with curly black hair, dark brown skin, and big round eyes that looked like an avocado cut in half. The child looked to be in third or fourth grade, I figured.

"Who are you and where do you come from?" Avocado Eyes demanded, prodding me in the chest with an unusually long finger.

"Uh, I'm Rose from Arizona."

"So you're not from here, then?" the child whispered, excited. Fleck just nodded back, a small smile on her face.

I shook my head. "I'm from a place very far away, I think."

All three of them looked to one another again, deciding which question to ask me next. I continued, "And who are you?"

The brick boy pointed to himself. "I'm Jonquil. That's Scape—they're a little ball of energy!"

"I'm Scape!" Scape held their hand out to me, grasping mine and shaking it.

"And you already know Fleck," Jonquil said.

I nodded at her. Fleck stared back at me with a deep and serious frown. "It's time we got down to business," she demanded. "She says that Jo gave her a Smoke Ball."

Jonquil and Scape looked at each other with shocked eyes.

"So it's true?" Jonquil asked.

"She's the one who will help us?" Scape added.

"I have my doubts. She doesn't even seem to know what an Islet is."

They both quirked their eyebrows at me, unimpressed.

"Look," I said, "I'll be honest with you. Jo's my aunt, and she did give me the watch—er, the *Smoke Ball*—but I can't help you with anything. I'm just a kid." The dream was more fun, I decided, if I went along with it. I would wake up soon enough anyway, and I preferred this place to the real world. Plus, there was something in me that tingled—thinking maybe it *could* be real.

Fleck looked genuinely confused. "She told us that she was training a replacement and that they would arrive soon. That's why we were looking all over the island for you."

"Training a replacement?" I thought about all the stories Jo had told me, all the hours we'd spent painting and drawing. It seemed that she had been preparing me for this world and its strange drawing powers. "I guess she did train me. She mostly just told me about the realms."

The three leaned in, their eyes wider than before.

"I knew it! Can you fly to the others?" Fleck said a bit too loudly. Jonquil grasped her by the shoulder, pulling her back.

"What do you mean 'fly'?" I asked.

"Jo was the only one of us who could fly over the Wall. Each of the hour worlds has a Wall, see, and because she could pass over them, she could go anywhere. Using the Smoke Ball," Scape explained. "She used to tell us fairy tales of those other places."

"They're not fairy tales, Scape. It's history," Jonquil said. "*They* just don't want you to know that."

"Who are 'they'?" I asked.

The three surrounded me in a half circle, and Fleck lowered her voice. "The Smoke Keepers," she said.

A shiver ran through me. Just hearing their name was frightening. Jo had told me that the Smoke Keepers like to steal magic from people and that there's a different Smoke Keeper in every world—but that's all I knew.

I didn't like when she told me stories about them; they scared me, so she didn't talk about the Smoke Keepers that often.

"We have a Smoke Keeper—he's horrible. He captures people and throws them into the Wall," Scape said.

"Why?" I asked.

"The Walls need smoke to stay up. They're made of smoke. So when a person is thrown into the Wall, all of that person's smoke is sucked out."

"Why don't people stop them?"

"Some people like the Smoke Keepers," Scape whispered, "because they keep order."

"And the rest of us are too afraid of getting thrown into the Wall," Fleck added.

"Jo told us all about the Smoke Keepers from other lands—they used to be the Kings and Queens of each hour world more than a hundred years ago," Jonquil said.

I remembered that part of the story—about the Kings and Queens. There were twelve worlds for each of the twelve hours. The worlds didn't use to be separated, but then the Kings and Queens decided to keep them apart. Jo had never told me why. She claimed that I would understand it when I got older.

"But how can the Kings and Queens still be alive?" I asked.

"They each created a Wall, and now they feed off it. They are living off the smoke that has been stolen from others. But they look like skeletons, because they aren't *really* alive and they aren't *really* dead," Jonquil said.

I imagined the thin face and empty eyes of Eleven's Smoke Keeper. He did look like a skeleton.

Jonquil continued, "The Smoke Keepers keep the Walls alive so that the twelve worlds will stay apart."

"Why did they want to separate them?" I said.

Scape wrung their hands as they looked at Jonquil. "We'll tell you at the end of the story."

"When we're *sure* we can trust you," Fleck added.

"Okay," I agreed. "But how do you get smoke out of someone?" I asked.

Scape plugged their nose and mouth and then breathed hard. A puff of green smoke shot out each of their ears. "It's easy, see?"

The three continued to explain, jumping back and forth.

Apparently, the Walls became so powerful that no one could cross them. In fact, if you got close, you got "Smoke Sick" as you breathed it in. If you lost all of your smoke, you died.

"But if you inhale too much smoke, you *also* die," Scape explained.

If people did really bad things, the Smoke Keeper of Eleven would toss them into the Wall. It would suck their smoke straight out.

"After you get sucked into the Wall, it takes five days, and then, poof, your body is gone," Scape said plainly.

"Can you pull them back out before then?" I asked.

"No. Once the Wall has you, it won't let go."

"But I thought you said you were going to destroy the Wall?" I asked, turning to Fleck, who grimaced.

"Well, we were supposed to, but we need to go to the other worlds to collect the necessary tools."

"Why didn't Jo destroy all the Walls, then?" I asked. "If all you have to do is go between worlds, then Jo could have done it, right?"

"It's not that simple." Jonquil sounded uneasy. "You have to collect smoke from each world *from* the Smoke Keeper of that realm."

"Jo wasn't very powerful," Fleck went on, "so she was afraid of getting caught by the Smoke Keepers in the other worlds."

"But you think I'm strong enough?"

They all looked at me like I had said something totally silly.

"Well, sure. She said that you had more smoke than any of us."

"Me? But I've never even used smoke!"

They looked at one another again, even more surprised. Jonquil leaned in to Fleck to whisper something. Fleck nodded, turning to me.

"Come close to me. I need to see your eyes."

I felt my cheeks burn. "My eyes? Why?"

"That's how you see how much smoke someone's got."

Fleck grabbed me by the shoulders. She was so close that I could feel her breath on my nose as she stared into my eyes.

"Wow" was all she said before releasing me. "She was right."

"Right? What do you mean 'right'?" I asked.

Jonquil snatched a small mirrored square off his belt and held it up in front of my eyes.

"You can tell how much smoke someone has, how strong they are, based on how many specks and lines they have in their eyes. It's just the way they're born."

"Your eyes are mostly specks!" Scape chirped. "And I thought I had specks." They batted their eyelids. From a distance I could see some dark green spots in their eyes.

I looked in the mirror. I don't like mirrors much. I think my face is boring, and my eyes definitely aren't special. As I looked at their reflection, they were the same dull hazel they'd always been. Looking closer, however, I saw the specks Scape was talking about.

My eyes weren't clear, like Jo's. They were speckled with lots of brown and green dots that shot through the irises in streaks. "Okay, so I see some colors and shapes. So what?"

"It means you have power." I looked up at Jonquil; I could see a couple big lines in his eyes. Fleck had lots of small dots, like her freckles.

"Well, where I come from, it just means they're *dirty*." That's what Jeremiah used to call my eyes, anyway.

Fleck sighed, holding my nose. "Blow."

I rolled my eyes but did as she said, keeping my mouth shut as Scape had done. I blew hard once and heard them gasp.

"What?" I pulled away to look around. A cloud of brown smoke descended on me, and I coughed. "Ack! What was that?"

"That's your smoke."

I squinted my eyes through the cloud. There did seem to be a lot of it—at least three times what Scape had had.

"Why is mine brown if Scape's is green?" I asked.

"That's what Jo's smoke looked like too. She said that's what the smoke from everyone in your world looks like."

"My world?"

Jonquil nodded. "She called it Thirteen."

I squinted hard. That was silly. Jo had never told me there were thirteen hours. "And what are the powers of people from Thirteen?" I asked.

I knew the powers of everyone from the twelve hours, based on Jo's nursery rhyme. They could turn into animals, float, draw ghostly objects, create fire, be super strong—you know, amazing things.

"You can travel to all of the other worlds and save us," Scape answered.

"Well, that's a boring power," I mumbled to myself. I think Fleck heard, though, because moments later she shoved a nail and a block of wood into my hand.

"Jo also said you could use all the other powers so long as you're in that world. So show us by drawing something."

I shrugged. Drawing was something I could do, no problem. "What should I draw?" I was reminded of asking Jo the same question.

"A bird."

I followed Fleck's pointing finger to see the fire bird's wings beating lazily. It had begun to flicker, as if the flame were nearly out.

The bird wasn't very big. It had a small head with a

short, rounded beak and a long tail that dipped down as it flew. It reminded me a bit of a trogon, a bird from where I'm from, with a bright red chest, a Christmas-green back, and silver wings.

I imagined a trogon as best I could. I hadn't seen many—they were shy, but I liked that about them. It made it all the more special when you did see one. I imagined the feathers on its wings separated and pointed as it flew, its body a line. I imagined what it would feel like to fly.

The nail scratched easily into the wood, shredding it into pleasantly small curls that fell to the ground as my hand moved feverishly. I was working quickly, as Jo had always demanded. But I wanted it to be good too. I wanted the others to know that I *could* draw.

"Okay. Finished." I spun the block around.

They were staring back, faces set. I heard Fleck gasp.

"Wha—"

The block had begun to glow with brown smoke. I dropped it suddenly, the carved side landing up. I had remembered the ship pouring from Fleck's fingers in the same way.

The brown energy shot from the middle of the block into the air, spinning, writhing, reforming into an unmistakable shape: the bird.

It trailed brown smoke and glowed so brightly that I could hardly look at it. The bird flew upward, spinning and thrashing as it soared to life. It was the same size as I drew it on the block.

Soon the grayish brown dissipated, making way for white wood underneath.

The other bird's wings clicked, wood on wood, as they flapped, sending the bird higher toward its flickering fire twin.

The two met in the center of a circle, colliding with a flash of light. The wooden bird had caught fire and was flying lazy circles around the room. The fire bird was gone.

I tore my eyes away from the scene to look at the three strangers in front of me. They were staring back with a look that I can only describe as flabbergasted.

I wanted to speak, wanted to ask if that had been what they were hoping for, but I couldn't push a single word from my throat. I looked down at my shaking hands. I had never felt such power before—and yet it had been so natural.

Did I really do that?

"That was . . ." I looked up at Jonquil, who was having trouble picking his words.

"Fantastic!" Scape said.

I couldn't help but smile. Very few people had ever said that to me. "Thanks."

With these three and Alejandro, maybe I'm not so alone after all.

Scape then looked at me, serious. "We'll tell you why the Walls are there," they sighed, turning to Fleck, as if asking her to finish.

Fleck complied. "It's because they want us dead."

"Wait, who wants you dead?" I asked.

"Everyone does," Fleck answered. "See, some of us have more than one kind of smoke."

"Our great-great-grandparents were from different worlds, so they had different powers," Jonquil continued. "That scares the Kings and Queens, because the three of us can do things that no one else can, so they think that, one day, we will overthrow them."

They showed me in turn. Jonquil drew a flower, but no matter what he drew it on, it appeared made of fire.

That means he has the powers of Eleven and Three, I thought, remembering Jo's nursery rhyme.

Scape could make things that were indestructible. That reminded me of Four's powers—the inhabitants were like cartoon characters who couldn't get hurt, like their bodies were made of rubber. So Scape was a mix of Eleven and Four.

Then Fleck showed me her powers again. She could draw something and then make it bigger or smaller. *She must be partly from Six,* I realized, where people can control the size of things.

"They got rid of most of the people with more than one power a hundred years ago," Jonquil explained, "and then they created the Walls to make sure no one can be born with multiple powers ever again."

"How were you three born, then?" I asked them.

"Well, a lot of us hide among everyone else, never showing our powers. If we do get found, then we're thrown into the Wall by the Smoke Keepers," Jonquil said with a shiver.

The image of the crackling Wall, swirling with energy—*with smoke*—shot in front of my memory.

Jonquil went on, his voice low. "People have been hiding for many years. My mother had two smokes, and my dad had one. Now I have a bit from both of them."

"Same as you," Fleck said, pointing at my chest, "brown smoke girl."

"Same as Jo," Scape added. "That's why she had to be careful. If you're not strong enough to fight a Smoke Keeper, then you have to hide."

"How did you find each other?" I asked.

"Jo found us. She's been keeping us safe. She said

that you would help us now." Scape looked up at me with hopeful eyes.

"You're the missing link, Rose from Arizona." Fleck held my hand in one of hers. I flushed. "Together we're powerful enough. We're going to destroy the Walls for good."

"What exactly do I have to do, though?"

"Jo already started. She got the smoke from five of the Smoke Keepers already."

"Which ones?"

"Look at the Smoke Ball. You'll see the different colors she's found."

I plucked the Smoke Ball from my pocket. When I looked closely, I noticed that it swirled with five different colors: yellow, white, violet, pink, and black.

"Which worlds did she go to?" I asked.

They looked at one another and Fleck shrugged. "She said that you would know."

I sighed. It seemed that Jo had left a lot of mysterious clues that I still didn't understand. I hoped she would come home soon and explain them.

"And what exactly are we going to do with the Smoke Ball once it has all the smokes in it? Just . . . throw it at the Wall?"

"Of course not." Fleck grinned, a mischievous glint

in her eyes. "We're going to fit it into this."

She scurried to one corner, lifting up a colorful pillow to reveal something long, wrapped in leather, underneath. She unfolded the leather to expose a gold sword.

It was plain and looked homemade, but very sturdy.

"Jo told us how to build it. She designed it based on old drawings. This was the sword wielded by the one King who fought against the rest. According to the legend, he was going to use his sword to destroy the Walls. Jonquil used his fire smoke to mold the metal into the exact shape."

"See," Jonquil said, excited. He pointed to a hole, exactly the size of the watch, in the hilt. "The Smoke Ball fits in there. Then the sword will be powered by smoke from all the Kings and Queens. It's the only thing powerful enough to destroy the Walls."

"Once the sword is ready, we'll take down the Walls for good."

"So . . . we're going to . . . stab a Wall?" I asked.

Fleck rolled her eyes. "I'm not certain Jo picked the right hero, after all." She wrapped the sword up, glowering at me as she replaced it under the long pillow.

"You'll have to teach me."

They all nodded at once. "We will," Scape promised.

"Good, because I—"

BOOM. BOOM. BOOM.

The sound was so loud that it shook the walls and floor, but only I seemed to notice. The three looked at me, confused.

"Rose?"

"She's disappearing like Jo does!"

BOOM. BOOM. BOOM.

It was like a pounding in my head that made my whole body vibrate. I could hardly move, let alone speak. I could feel someone put their hand on my shoulder.

"...meet us tomorrow. We'll find you and together—"

I could just barely make out Fleck's voice as my vision swam in and out, blackness appearing to the beat of the pounds.

BOOM. BOOM—

THE FRIEND

"Rose? Are you in there?"

The words swirled into my mind; I was still clinging to the dream. Then I realized someone was knocking on the church door.

I had only a few seconds to sit up before it creaked open. I saw a shaggy head poke in. "Rose? Oh, cool! I thought you'd still be here."

"Alejandro," I croaked, my voice still filled with sleep. "What time is it?"

If it was super late, Mom would freak out.

"School is about to end. I came by during lunch, but you were still asleep. I didn't want to wake you up, but I wanted to make sure you didn't sleep through the final bell, so I snuck out early."

He came in here and saw me asleep? And had I really

been asleep that long? The dream felt way shorter.

"Oh, uh, thanks." I stood up, feeling awkward as I patted down my clothes. I felt the watch in my fist and quickly slid it into my pants pocket.

When I looked down, however, to see if the chain was safely tucked inside, I saw something strange on my palm.

"Okay, well, I'm glad you're awake, I've got to—"

"Wait!"

He swung around, surprised, as I rushed toward him.

"Yeah?"

I shoved my hand up to his face. I knew my eyes probably looked wide and wild.

"What's this? Do you see this?"

He squinted at my palm. "Uh, it looks kind of like . . . like the letter *C*. Why?"

I looked down. Sure enough, there was a thin *C* carved into my skin—right where the Smoke Keeper had cut me. It wasn't bleeding, like it had been in Eleven, but it was definitely there, raised and pale pink.

Alejandro was still staring at me warily. I looked back at him.

"What would you do if I told you"—I sucked in a deep breath—"that there is a . . . a whole other *universe* with *magic*?" I shouldn't have said it. It was like I was trying to ask myself.

I expected him to laugh, to convince me it was impossible, but instead—

"Of course there is."

"Wait, what?"

Alejandro shrugged. "It's like space, right? There have got to be smart aliens out there on another planet *somewhere*, so I bet there's also another reality with magic too. There's, like, infinite realities, according to *Warp Jump 3000*."

His words zoomed through my ears, none of them sticking. "What are you talking about?"

"*Warp Jump 3000*! It's a game about alternate realities!" Excited, he sat down on a pew, pulling his tablet out of his bag. I sat next to him.

He clicked on an app from his never-ending list of games. This one was mostly just stick figures and words. A line of text scrolled across the tablet: OF THE INFINITE UNIVERSES THAT SURROUND US AT ALL TIMES . . . THIS . . . IS ONE OF THEM. Then the screen was swallowed by a black hole that was replaced by a world where tiny stick people ran around with candies for heads. I'm not entirely sure what the point of the game was or why Alejandro had it. He seemed to like it, though, as he furiously tapped the screen as he spoke.

"How does this prove that magic exists?" I asked.

"Well, because if you can think of something, then it must exist in a reality somewhere. That's what the game says, anyway. Ha! Gotcha, sucker!" he screamed as he squashed a running lollipop.

"How would someone travel into a fantasy world?"

"I guess," he replied, pausing the game, "if it was in another dimension, then they could teleport, like in *Warp Jump*, or they could get there through astral projection. I have an X-Men game where Jean Grey astral projects."

"What does that mean?"

"Well, when you teleport, your whole body actually moves—like, the atoms just, poof, disappear, then they reappear somewhere else. Astral projection, though, is when it's just your *mind* that reappears somewhere else."

"So just my . . . brain is going into the other world? Like a dream . . . but real?"

"Exactly!"

"But if it was just my brain going into another world, then if I got hurt there, would I still be hurt when I woke up?"

"Hmm, that's an interesting question." Alejandro

scrolled through his games, pulling up an X-Men app. "In the astral projection game, if someone gets hurt, they don't, like, stay hurt. Like, if you get stabbed, you don't die, but it would still hurt."

"It would?" I asked, rubbing the *C*.

"Sure, because you'd have mental pain. Your brain would think you were hurt still, so it would send pain signals to your nerves."

"Could the place you got stabbed get, like, swollen?" I asked, feeling the raised lines.

"I guess if your brain thought that you were hurt, it could still make it swollen even if your body wasn't *actually* stabbed."

I nodded quickly. My heart was racing so fast. *It's possible. The world might be real.*

"Why do you ask?" Alejandro looked up at me, storing the tablet again.

"Oh, uh, I just had a dream, and it gave me an idea for a . . . game."

"Wait, really? Can I help? I've always wanted to design a game!" He stood up, bouncing on his heels. He looked genuinely excited. I almost felt guilty.

"Sure, yeah, sounds good," I said, grabbing my stuff quickly as I tried to control my breathing, rubbing a thumb over my palm again.

The world is real. It's real.

The two of us walked out. As Alejandro babbled about other worlds and time warps and phantom pain, I just focused on not shaking the watch in my pocket too much.

There was a whole world in there.

THE BATTLE OF THE SLUMBER PARTY

I felt bad lying about where I was all day when Mom came to pick me up, but she soon got distracted when I told her about Jo.

"Oh, bubala, I heard. But we'll find her, I know we will."

I told her about the hospital, and Wes, and Cindy. I didn't tell her about the watch or the dreamworld, though. I was realizing how important Jo's rules were.

We drove home. Which, for now, was on the second story of the Shooting Star, an apartment building that used to be a motel. It was a lot smaller than Wes's house, but it felt way more like home.

We ate at the dining room table, which squeaked when you leaned on it. Mom didn't have time to cook, but she said it was a good thing that she worked at a diner because it meant that she could bring home the best food in all of Arizona. I liked that she worked at a diner because I could have a grilled cheese every night.

Usually I liked dinner because it was the only time I really got to talk to someone, but today all I was thinking about was the watch, heavy in my pocket. I couldn't wait until it was 11:00 and I could go see my new friends again.

Real friends.

The very thought made me smile.

"What are you smiling about?" Mom teased, nudging me with a fry.

I rolled my eyes. I had to be more careful. "Oh, nothing. Just, you know, school."

"Oh yeah? You don't usually smile about school. Did something happen?" She wiggled her eyebrows at me.

I tried to keep my face blank, but she knew that always made me laugh. It looked like her eyebrows were fighting caterpillars.

"Not really, just a funny day."

"Well, I'm glad you're being so brave about Jo, then."

I know she meant it in a nice way, but the words thumped hard. *Oh yeah, I guess I shouldn't be so happy about the watch world. Jo is still missing. I should be worried about her.*

I think Mom saw my face go dark because she

nudged me again. "I didn't mean that you should be sad. What is it—did you make new friends?"

"No!" I said too quickly, thinking about Fleck, Scape, and Jonquil.

"Ooh, is it a boy?"

"*No!*" I said even more quickly, remembering Alejandro. I knew if I mentioned him that Mom would get excited about me having a—ugh—*boy*friend. (She called any boy who was my friend a "boyfriend." She used to do that with Jeremiah. It was humiliating.) Why couldn't I just be friends with a boy, anyway? Why did it have to mean something else? Why did she never call my girl friends, *girl*friends? "I just . . . really like what we're studying in class, is all. It's alternate universes. Really cool stuff."

"Oh." I could hear the drop in Mom's voice. "I suppose that's nice too. I was just hoping perhaps you were making some new friends."

"Who needs friends?" I asked, stabbing a fry a bit too hard into a puddle of ketchup.

I didn't have to look up to know that Mom was doing her sad smile. I hated her sad smile, especially when it was because of me.

"One day you'll meet someone who understands how special you are."

"Jo thinks I'm special."

"Maybe someone a bit younger than Jo."

I sighed. "I wouldn't hold your breath."

Mom chuckled. "See? You're great. Just trust me— when all those silly kids get a bit older, they will realize that being different is actually a terrific thing. Then they will all want to be just like you."

I snorted to myself, thinking about Jeremiah and Fallon wearing baggy plaid hoodies and dirty jeans while painting nerdy fantasy worlds in a haunted church.

Then I thought of Alejandro.

Hey, actually, that doesn't seem so far off . . .

My phone buzzed with a new text. It was sitting on the side of the table nearer Mom. She leaned over to read the message as it flashed onto the screen. "Oh, maybe it's about Jo, did your dad—"

Mom had gone silent, her hand over her mouth.

I felt the adrenaline rise. *Did they find her?*

"What? Mom? You're scaring me."

She suddenly broke into a wide grin and flipped the phone around so I could read it. "You, my wonderful Rose, are going to a *slumber party* tonight!"

"Huh?" I felt my stomach plummet as I read the text message:

Fallon Berg: Hey, Rosmary, plz come to my birthday slumber party tonight. My house. ;) Xoxoxo

That didn't sound like the Fallon I knew.

But do I even know her anymore?

"And it's at Fallon's house! Remember when you two were the cutest little BFFs? Oh, I'm so happy she's back in your life. I knew you were happy about more than just class. I knew it. Okay, now let me find your cutest pj's . . ."

"Wait, Mom." I stood up quickly, snatching my phone from her. "I'm not going."

Mom's smile slipped off, and her brows creased up. "What?"

"I—I just . . ." This had to be some kind of prank. Fallon wouldn't have spelled my name wrong like that. There was no way I was going to her house. She wouldn't even speak to me at school. Worse, Jeremiah would be there. "I can't. I have a lot of homework."

Plus, I have to go back to Eleven tonight.

"On a Friday night? Rose, stop worrying about school so much. Having fun is just as important." Mom grabbed me by the shoulders, rubbing my arms. Of course she wanted me to go.

Ugh, what a disaster. If she hadn't seen it, I could have just ignored the message.

"But, Mom—"

"No buts! Do you remember how much you cried

when Fallon didn't invite you to her back-to-school party? Well, now she *is* inviting you! Let's just take the good moments when we can. Now, seriously, where are those plaid pj's? I remember I washed them—"

"I don't really know Fallon anymore. She doesn't even like me."

"Wait a minute, Rosemary." I flinched at the use of my full name. "You do this all the time—insulting yourself and pretending no one likes you—but this young lady just invited you to her birthday party. You want friends, I know you do, and I will not allow you to just ignore people when they finally realize how great you are."

I sighed. I wasn't going to be able to convince her, but this . . . this was a *nightmare*.

"Please, Mom—"

"No. No excuses. You are going, and that's the end of it. Here"—Mom thrust her lucky backpack into my hands, the one she used only when she had big tests because she didn't like to get it dirty—"fill this with your clothes and a toothbrush. We have to leave in three minutes so that I can drop you off and still get to my class."

I looked down at the backpack. There was no way out.

"Okay?" she asked again.

I just nodded.

I couldn't wait for 11:00 so that I could escape.

By the time we pulled up to Fallon's house, I thought maybe, *just maybe*, Fallon had actually invited me because she wanted to. Mom seemed pretty certain of it.

"I knew she'd come around one day. She always looked up to you, I know it. Remember how you used to make her laugh?"

But as we pulled up in the Dino-Wagon (that's what I'd named Mom's car—it was big, ancient, and the paint was peeling off like scales), I saw three girls' faces giggling from Fallon's bedroom window. As soon as I looked at them, they laughed harder and pulled their heads back into the room.

Well, this is going to be terrible, I thought as I opened the Dino-Wagon's heavy door.

"Christine! How are you?"

"Martha! George! It's been forever!"

Mom rushed up to Fallon's parents. I knew they weren't her favorite people in the whole world. Mom was kind of a hippie, with long, messy black hair that she liked to tie up in a bun and big brown eyes that she ringed with smudgy black pencil. The Bergs, on the other hand, looked like they should be on TV. When

Fallon was my best friend, when Mom and Dad were going through the divorce, I used to ask Mr. and Mrs. Berg if they would be my parents too. As I looked at Mom standing next to them now, I felt guilty. She was the best. If only she hadn't made me come over here, that is.

I trudged up to the three of them, listening in on the conversation.

"... we were surprised too when we heard Rosemary was coming," Mr. Berg was saying.

"Pleasantly surprised!" Mrs. Berg interjected, smiling widely at me.

I smiled back. I thought we probably both looked fake.

"Why don't you go in, hon, and say hi to your friends?" Mom nudged me toward the front door.

"Okay," I mumbled. It was pretty much the last thing I wanted to do, but I knew Mom had to leave to go to class anyway. I didn't want to cause her any trouble or make her late.

The house itself was just as I remembered it. I knew every hallway and every room—and there were a lot of them. I stood in front of Fallon's bedroom door.

It looked different.

It used to be bright pink and covered in drawings we

had done together and stickers from *The Blossoms*, our favorite cartoon, but now it was white with one giant poster of Hyung-Gyun, the rapper from that boy band that everyone at school liked.

Where's the pink? Her favorite color is pink.

I could hear faint voices on the other side of the door. I didn't really want to listen, but it was like a magnet was pulling me closer.

"I can't believe how fast she got here."

". . . still in those same clothes?"

"It's going to be so funny and—"

I took another step forward.

"Shh! I heard something."

My hand froze on the handle, and my heart sent ripples through my body.

"Is someone there?" a voice called from inside.

I pushed the door open, but I couldn't bear to raise my gaze from the carpet. I felt just as scared here as I had facing off against the Smoke Keeper in Eleven.

I heard giggles again, then more shushing.

"You guys, stop."

That's Fallon.

I looked up, and sure enough, Fallon was shaking her head at the seven other girls. She looked back at me for only a second before rolling her eyes to the ground too.

"Rosemary! You made it!" Helene Grossmont sang.

More giggles. There must have been some really great joke that I didn't know.

"Thanks for inviting me," I mumbled.

Laughter followed, which made me blush. I knew I hadn't done anything wrong, but I felt like I had.

"Stop being weird and just sit down," one girl sneered. That was Samantha Plank. She had curly brown hair and three ear piercings. I don't think she ever liked me much.

I shuffled away from the door. They were all sitting in a circle, but there was no room to join, so I sat alone just outside of it, my backpack still strapped on.

I knew instantly that this was going to be one of the longest nights of my life, but I was trapped. The more I tried to distance myself from them, the more they got mad, but then the more I tried to join in, the more they made fun of me.

The only person who didn't seem to care about me at all was Fallon. Since I'd entered the room, she had looked at me only once.

I decided the safest bet was to remain outside the circle.

All night long I heard Jo's voice in my head, warning me how to stay alive in the face of monsters. *The less you show, the less they know.*

Jo had been talking about magical abilities, battle plans, secrets. In this sort of battle, though, you had to hide your feelings and how much it hurt when people said mean things.

I was still huddled on the floor while everyone else lounged on the bed and couch watching some movie about a girl becoming a mermaid.

The movie didn't seem unrealistic anymore after what I'd seen.

My hand closed around the watch in my pocket. I would never be alone if I had it with me. It was like a small piece of Jo was there too. She would protect me.

At least Jeremiah isn't here. That would be really—

"Grossy Rosey! What are you doing here? Don't you have a gross, dirty hole to sleep in?"

I couldn't even look at him as he walked in. I'm sure, judging by all the laughter around me, he was smiling pretty big.

"What are you doing here, *Jeremiah*?"

"Um, I don't know, *Fallon*. Maybe I'm hanging out in *my* house on *my* birthday?"

I looked up. The movie was paused, and the twins were nose to nose, glaring.

"Yeah, but your party isn't until tomorrow night *for a reason*. Today's *my* day."

Jeremiah looked straight at me. "Yeah, but Mom said I could hang out with you guys too." He waved. I ignored him.

"Let's play Truth or Dare!" Samantha shouted.

Everyone formed a circle on the ground. I stayed where I was, just outside of it.

"Come on Gros—"

Fallon slapped Jeremiah on the leg.

"I mean, *Rosemary*. Join us."

"I'm all right, thanks."

I expected him to keep bugging me, but to my surprise he gave in, turning to Samantha next to me.

"Okay, fine. Then, Sam—truth or dare?"

"Uh"—she glanced around, a bit nervous—"dare."

"I dare you to do an armpit fart."

"What?" she asked, already blushing as the other girls laughed loudly.

"Come on! Fart!" Jeremiah closed a hand around his armpit, pumping his elbow up and down.

"I don't know h—"

"Do it! Do it! Do it!" Jeremiah started the chant, but nearly everyone joined until Samantha gave in.

They laughed harder.

It went around like this. Embarrassing truths: "Who do you have a crush on?" "When was the last time you peed your pants?" "Who is your best friend here?" And even more embarrassing dares: "Tell Fallon's dad you love him." "Do the chicken dance." "Crawl around and cry like a baby."

As I looked on, I realized that if this is what it meant to have friends, I didn't know if I ever wanted them. People saying and doing things against their wishes. There was something icky about it, like something had crawled under their skin and made them do things they didn't want to. Everyone laughed except for the person being laughed at.

Finally, the circle came around to me.

"All right, Rosey, your turn."

I mumbled, refusing to look up, "No, thanks."

"It's not an option, *Rosemary*," Samantha said, hands on her hips. "If you're here, you have to play. It's Fallon's birthday."

"I don't want to." My voice was quiet. I wished I could be louder.

"Do it, Rosey!"

"Do it! Do it! Do it!"

My heart was beating so fast. They wouldn't leave me alone.

"It's fine. I don't even care. Who's next?" Fallon interrupted.

I sighed, relieved. The Fallon I knew was still in there, somewhere. I tried to smile at her, a thank-you smile, but she didn't even meet my eye.

"Fine, then," Jeremiah snapped. "Samantha, truth or dare?"

"Truth," she replied quickly.

"Who here is the biggest loser?"

"Rosemary."

Giggles.

"Helene, truth or dare?"

"Truth."

"Who here has the ugliest clothes?"

"Rosemary."

"Justine, what's the worst thing about Rosemary?"

He continued asking everyone the same question, and the answers came faster each time.

"She's so quiet, it's creepy."

"She thinks she's smarter than everyone else."

"Her mom is so embarrassing."

Jeremiah then talked to himself. "Um, Jeremiah? Truth or dare? Truth." Everyone laughed as he continued, "Who doesn't belong here?"

Seven of the girls, all except Fallon, cried, "Rosemary!"

Although I had said worse stuff about myself, hearing these things from other people stung so much more.

It hurt worse because everyone else could hear it.

Fallon could hear it.

"Fallon, truth or dare?"

"This is a dumb game. Why don't we do something else?"

"Nuh-uh, truth or dare?"

"Fine, then. *Dare.*"

"Okay." Jeremiah had completely taken over the game. He turned to me with a grin. I wanted to run away, but there was nowhere to go. "I dare you to tell Rosemary why you aren't friends anymore."

"I told you this is dumb!" Fallon shouted at him, standing suddenly.

"Oh! I can answer!" Samantha shouted, raising her hand. "It's because Rosemary was, like, obsessed with her, right?"

My heart was beating faster and faster. I couldn't even speak. *This really is a nightmare.*

"Rosemary started drawing all of the time because Fallon was good at it."

That's not true.

"And she would follow her around everywhere."

We were best friends.

"I heard she cried the last time she wasn't invited to her party."

"She put her hair in a ponytail because that's what Fallon did."

"I heard she told her that she *loved* her."

I did.

I do.

They were talking so fast, excited to say the exact things that cut me the deepest.

"If you guys don't stop making fun of people, then I'm leaving!" Fallon's face was bright red. "It's my birthday, and I just wanted to have fun. I knew you'd do this, that's why I didn't want to invite her in the first place."

That, somehow, was the worst thing anyone had said all night. I felt the tears prickle at the corners of my eyes.

I have to get out. Why am I even here?

Everyone just giggled. They tried to calm Fallon down with comments like "It's fine" and "We're just joking."

Fallon finally sat back down.

"If you didn't invite her, then who did?" Jeremiah asked, scowling.

"Me," Samantha said with a grin. "It was just a prank. I can't believe you actually came." She looked at me, but I didn't want to look back. "You can go home whenever you want, you know."

No, I can't. Mom's in class until late.

"All right, all right, all right—that's enough," Jeremiah cut in, standing between the girls. "Sorry, Rosey. It was just supposed to be funny. We didn't mean it."

"Yeah, we didn't mean it," a few voices agreed.

"And we'll leave you alone forever, I promise, if you play the game just once." He leaned in toward me. I felt totally defenseless. I was tired and I wanted to cry.

"Truth or dare?"

I knew I shouldn't answer, but I hoped that maybe if I did, it would finally be over.

"Truth."

He squatted in front of me, meeting my eyes.

"Is it true that you like my sister?"

"Jeremiah! Stop it!" I heard Fallon shout.

There were shrieks and laughs in response. But that was it. That was enough.

I stood up and rushed from the room, past Mr. Berg, who was about to bang on the door. "Quiet down, kids, it's—oh! Rosemary, where are you . . . ?"

But I was gone. I ran through the halls, down the stairs, and into the basement. It was filled with old furniture and games. *This* is where we used to have sleepovers.

Fallon would know where I'd gone, but maybe no one else would. Maybe they would leave me alone now.

I lay down on an old, flowery couch that squeaked when I moved. Tears leaked out of my eyes. I couldn't stop them.

I want to go home. I want to go home so bad.

Even if Mom wasn't in class, I didn't want her to know that I had failed.

Between Jo going missing and this disaster of a party, it was the worst day of my life.

Then I felt something warm in my pocket. I stuck my hand in and retrieved the watch.

Suddenly excited, I clicked it open. It was already past 10:00. I just had to wait an hour to see my new friends.

I watched the hands, becoming sleepier with every spin, forgetting about the party, Jeremiah, Fallon.

None of it mattered, not compared to the world inside the watch.

"Is it true that you like my sister?"

Jeremiah's words swam in my head as everything became fuzzy with sleep.

Not anymore, I had wanted to say.

The second the hands hit 11:00, I pushed the sharp

thoughts away. I imagined the graveyard and the pure white catacombs.

The ghosts of whispers, footsteps, and giggles surrounded me, but I had already given in to sleep.

ELEVEN

This time when I woke, I was right outside the graveyard, the catacombs rising behind me as thick, marble cubes of white, hiding me from the rest of the town. The rest of Eleven.

I guess when I imagine a specific place, that's where I end up? I thought, blinking.

"You actually came! We took rotations just to make sure no one else found you first! Ha!"

I was lying in the dirt, looking up at the sky. My head hurt and my eyes felt puffy.

I squinted up. The sun was low, but it speared through the branches of a tree and nailed me in the eyes. I could barely see the big pink boy crouching over me.

"That was a good trick, friend," Jonquil said.

He reached a strong arm out to me. I took his hand, and he lifted me up as if I were a doll.

"What?"

"Just *pop*—appearing out of nowhere like that! What do you call that? Popping? Zapping? *Kablamming*?"

"It's just . . . astral projecting, I guess." *Or teleporting, maybe*, I thought, remembering Alejandro's words.

He stopped, peering at me with a slightly disappointed look. "Huh," he mumbled, then he started brushing me off. "Well, we can work on a better name."

As we walked, I slowly remembered everything that had happened that night.

I wonder what's going on at Fallon's house. Have they found me? I got too nervous to even think about it. *Man. My life has gotten* weird *this week.*

Jonquil was so tall and his shoulders were so wide that when I walked behind him, I was completely covered in shadow.

I followed him, trudging through swampy ground. The mud was thick and wet and covered in green slime—it was also much deeper than I thought it would be. When I stepped down into it, I sank halfway up to my calf.

"It's a little . . . hard to walk," I shouted after him,

though he was doing just fine. He turned back to look at me just as I stomped down hard, sending algae rolling across the mud.

"Wait! Stop!" he yelled, splashing toward me and pointing to the green slime. "Watch out for the Grogs."

"What's a—"

And then I saw them. It wasn't algae at all. The little slimy balls were actually tiny creatures—bulbous and squishy—that hopped away from me, scared and fast, as I plowed through. The closer I looked, the more I realized that what had seemed like rolling waves across the surface of the swamp were actually fleeing swarms of bright green Grogs.

We walked forward—but now I was looking much closer at the mud. I followed Jonquil's path, avoiding trampling any unsuspecting animals.

This place is so much nicer than the real world, I thought. Even with all its monsters, everything about it was so magical and interesting. *Maybe I'll just never go back to the real world. This could be my true home.* The thought came easy, as if Jo herself were whispering in my ear.

"Uh-oh." Jonquil stopped suddenly, pulling a chain out from under his shirt.

"What is it?"

He was looking down at his necklace—three bulbs on a chain. One was filled with purple smoke, one with green, and one with brown. The purple smoke was glowing. He winced, lifting it off his chest as if it burned.

"That's Fleck. We have to go."

"What do you mean?"

"This is her smoke. It only lights up like this when she's using a lot of it at once," he answered, tossing me a thin brown mask from his pocket. "Quick, put this on. We're entering the city."

"Where is she?"

But he didn't answer, throwing on a green mask of his own and breaking into a fast run. I followed as closely as I could, my short legs having to do twice the work of his long ones.

We tore across the cemetery and then through the city, where the revelries of the party had not ended, where two kids running as fast as they could hardly seemed strange.

"Look at the cute itty-bitty!" A woman dancing in the street grabbed my hand to spin me as we ran past, but Jonquil pulled me away.

"We don't have time! The smoke is getting hotter!"

He ran up metal stairs, all the way to a building stack. I followed, out of breath.

We skidded across the roof. My foot slipped, and he caught me. It would have been a long fall.

We kept running—down a fire escape, then up another building.

We were avoiding the party. I could see guards in the street. They wore the same yellow velvet of the Smoke Keeper, but they weren't as tall, thin, or scary. They did carry long sticks with pointy knives at the end, though.

I realized it was better that we were up on top of the buildings and out of sight than on the ground near the guards.

We didn't stop running until we reached the cliffs overlooking the Mire. From there it was obvious where we had to go.

A group of people had gathered on the shore. I could hear the hum of their chatter from all the way up.

"No good, no good" was all Jonquil muttered before beginning his rapid descent down the cliff's face. He expertly slid and hopped over the crevices. I followed but was far clumsier. I was tired, too, breathing hard. I didn't run that much in PE.

By the time I hit the beach, Jonquil was gone and the crowd had grown much louder. "Jonquil!" I shouted, but I didn't think he could hear me.

I weaved my way through the gigantic forms of the

sleeping Islets. As I reached the crowd, growing wider by the second, I managed to hear snippets of what they said.

". . . just appeared!"

". . . angry-looking thing."

"Is it dangerous?"

". . . Smoke Keeper is on his way."

The last one shot me through the chest. *The Smoke Keeper? Here?*

Fleck's warnings about being spirited away had chilled my blood, and I didn't want anything like that to happen to my new friends.

I tried to tune in to what everyone was saying:

"They say it has *different* magic."

"But how? Those kinds of people don't exist anymore, do they?"

Oh no.

A wave of panic hit me. Someone *had* found Fleck.

I forced myself through the crowd until I collided with a wide back.

Rubbing my head, I looked up, half expecting to see the Smoke Keeper. Instead, it was Jonquil, staring wide-eyed.

And in the middle of the circle of people was the last person I would have expected.

"Jeremiah?"

He wore a baggy T-shirt and sweatpants. *Pajamas?*

"Do you know this . . . *thing*?" The question came from a tall, round-bellied man who was holding Jeremiah in place—kneeling on the ground, his hands behind his back. He looked up at me, wincing. His face clouded in confusion and anger.

"Rosemary? I'm dreaming about *Rosemary*? Ugh." He spat on the ground between tired, heaving breaths.

Wow, Jeremiah can recognize me even when I'm wearing a mask. Do bullies have radar for me or something?

"So, you do know him?" the man snarled at me. I took a step back. I was unable to speak, unable to break my eyes away from Jeremiah.

How is he even here? Unless . . .

Then I spotted the thin line of swirling energy trailing from his left pants pocket.

The watch chain.

I felt my pocket for where the watch should have been, but it was empty. My heart pounded.

Oh no. Did he steal it from me at the slumber party?

The very idea that he might have taken it, laid even a single finger on it, filled me with anger. Jo had left it to me, trusted me with it.

"Grab her, too."

A woman in a long-tailed coat tried to snatch my arm, but Jonquil stepped between us. He pretended it was an accident as he gazed upward, hand over his eyes, looking at something. A second bulb on his necklace had begun to glow a faint green.

"I'm not his fr-friend, I swear," I stuttered, backing away from the oncoming townspeople.

Jeremiah, even with his hands behind his back, snorted, "Well, *that's* for sure."

The agreement seemed to pacify the crowd some, though they continued to loom over me. I glanced at Jonquil, who was looking at me from the corner of his eye. The rounded muscle of his arm twitched, tense.

"Who is he, then?"

"He appeared on the beach out of nowhere!"

"I saw him causing a ruckus!"

"Who is he?"

They were all staring at me. The whole crowd, quiet, waiting, growing.

"He's, um . . . uh . . . I don't know," I finally said, tearing my eyes away from his crouched form.

A hushed murmur shot through the crowd. I hoped they believed me. Even if Jeremiah was really here, he would wake up and be fine, but if I somehow outed

Jonquil, Scape, or Fleck, they were bound to be in a lot more trouble. We just had to stick it out until one of us woke—at least, I hoped I could wake up.

Can I return home without the watch?

My panic was interrupted by Jeremiah.

"Why would I dream about *you*? Seriously? I went to bed to get away from all you dumb girls." Jeremiah was glaring at me from the ground. Even here he was insufferable.

"It appears as though he knows you, does it not?"

At the very sound of that voice, the skin on my back began to prickle, sending tingles up and down my spine. It was him. The Smoke Keeper.

"Ew! He's even grosser than Rosey!"

The Smoke Keeper looked away from me and to Jeremiah. I scuttled backward. He approached him swiftly. Even Jeremiah looked frightened by the Smoke Keeper, though he recovered just as quickly.

"You don't scare me. Hear that? This is *my* dream."

The Smoke Keeper's head rotated to me, expression remaining exactly the same.

"A dream. Is that right?" He turned to the boy. "You're not from here, are you?"

The crowd had remained silent, but a quiet whisper rose as soon as Jeremiah spoke.

"From this stupid place? Yeah, no. I'm from the real world."

"Interesting, interesting, interesting . . ."

The Smoke Keeper walked to me, the knobs of his knees and elbows jutting out like a bird's. I backed away from him, heart hammering in my chest.

Wake up.

He leaned over me, eyes staring into mine. He wheezed a rattling breath.

Jo's warning sounded in my brain: *"All you hear is a long death rattle, and then it's too late."*

"People aren't supposed to come here from *other worlds.*"

The whispers intensified.

The Smoke Keeper reached out a bony hand, but I kept backing away.

He didn't follow me. Instead, he turned to Jeremiah, who was screaming, "All you freaks better let me go!"

"Thank you. I will take that boy now."

The Smoke Keeper took Jeremiah's hands, holding them in a vice grip. His face now pale, Jeremiah fought to rip his arms away.

"Whoa—I said, *let me go.*"

But he was no match for the Smoke Keeper, who hauled him over one shoulder, then saluted to the crowd. "Thank you all ever so much for your service. The Wall will be fed today."

The crowd saluted back to him in a mass of raised hands, many adjusting the masks on their faces as if to make certain they were still there.

The Smoke Keeper turned, giving me one last look with a smile, his long yellow teeth ending in their jagged points. Then he turned, yanking Jeremiah after him.

A sick little feeling of satisfaction tickled my stomach as I watched Jeremiah kick and scream, unable to get away from the Smoke Keeper's tight grip as he dragged him up the mountain.

Then I felt Jonquil bend down to my ear, whispering. "Quick, think of something. We have to save him."

Ugh, let the Smoke Keeper have him, I wanted to say. He would probably wake up the next morning after a well-deserved nightmare.

But what if he doesn't wake up? What if the Smoke Keeper does kill him?

I stared up at Jonquil, feeling helpless. He didn't look back, only winced, clutching at the purple bulb.

Then he looked down at me with a half smile. "Never mind. I think they heard."

"What—"

But before I could even finish my thought, I heard

the scream. I spun around to see a large, glowing green orb falling from the sky. As it came closer, I saw there was a person crouched inside.

"Scape!"

I nearly ran for them when I felt Jonquil pull me back. "Just wait."

Scape plummeted, surrounded by a glowing energy sphere, and was heading straight for the Smoke Keeper—no, the cliff behind him. The Smoke Keeper stopped to look, Jeremiah still kicking and screaming over his shoulder.

"Now!" I couldn't hear Scape well, but I could see the shape of their mouth and hear the dulled shout as they raised a finger and closed their eyes.

Moments before Scape hit the ground, I saw a bronze shape soaring above. It looked like a large bird with wide, sharp wings that glinted in the sun.

From it shot what looked to be an arrow, glowing purple.

That must be Fleck.

As it soared through the air, however, the glow dissipated and the arrow grew larger and larger.

In the last seconds onlookers fled toward the city, but the Smoke Keeper was trapped below the cliffside.

Boom.

The tip of the massive arrow, as thick as a light post, connected with Scape's shield, sending the sphere flying at the cliff. There was a mighty crack when Scape hit the rock, then the cliff began to slide. Big rocks were falling to the ground, straight toward Jeremiah and the Smoke Keeper.

"We have to get Scape," I whispered.

"They're fine," Jonquil said.

I watched, unable to move, as the dust settled at the base of the cliff. I heard a cough. Then someone stood.

It was Jeremiah, his eyes wide and hair sticking up every which way. He looked like a baby bird that had fallen out of a tree.

Normally, I would have laughed, but then another figure rose beside him. The Smoke Keeper's neck was bent at a funny angle, like it was broken, and his left foot was turned . . . backward.

Crack. He snapped his neck into place with a turn of his head.

Slam. He kicked his foot against the rock, spinning it back around.

Then he wheezed a rattling breath, blue smoke pouring from his mouth.

He really isn't alive, is he? This one-hundred-year-old monster can't be killed.

"Jeremiah! Run!"

Jeremiah heard me and took a step, but the Smoke Keeper shot a hand forward, grabbing him. From a deep, low voice in his throat, he growled, "The Wall is hungry."

But before they could get away again, the bronze bird swooped down, crashing into the Smoke Keeper.

Fleck leaped off the bird's back as it exploded in purple smoke.

"Go, go, go!"

Fleck, carrying a tired Scape, ran forward, followed closely by me, Jonquil, and Jeremiah.

"This is so weird!" Jeremiah yelled.

"Just do whatever I tell you, okay?" I shouted as we ran.

But as soon as we reached the edge of the shore, we saw that the entire city was blocked by a line of soldiers, their bayonets pointed right at us.

We were trapped.

"Worst dream ever!" Jeremiah squealed.

Meanwhile, Fleck handed Scape to Jonquil, then snatched a white tile block from her belt. She carved quickly.

I heard Jeremiah's gasp as purple light flooded out from the center of the block. A small boat appeared, outlined in glowing purple. It grew larger and larger until it looked like a real boat, made from all white.

"Come on!" Jonquil pushed me from behind. I stumbled toward the boat. We clambered on. The ship bobbed into the Mire.

I looked back to see a crowd of guards carrying something large and shadowy, but I hardly had time to watch as our boat rocked from side to side. I worried it might spill us into the boiling water below.

"Stop that! What do you think you're doing?" Fleck shouted.

I spun around to see Jeremiah trying to jump over the side of the boat, Fleck wrestling with him.

"You're going to get us all killed!" she said.

"I have to wake up!" he screamed back. "Let go!"

"Stop!" I hollered. "I can explain!" I grabbed Jeremiah by the shoulders, pulling him farther onto the ship. "This place isn't a dream, Jeremiah, it's real."

"Yeah, okay," he said, rolling his eyes as he turned back to the lip of the boat.

"No, really," I said, yanking him toward me. "You took my watch, didn't you?"

Jeremiah spun around to face me. "Is that what this is about? Am I dreaming about you because I feel guilty? Look, I didn't even draw on your face like everyone else did. I just saw the watch on the ground, and, well, you know, it was in my house! Finders keepers!"

He tried to pull away again, but I snatched his arm.

"Stop. Listen to me," I ground out. I was never this brave in the real world, but somehow here, with my hands firmly upon him—one push away from the burning Mire—I felt powerful.

Then I pinched his cheek with my nails. Hard.

"Ow! What is your problem?"

"Can you usually feel pain in a dream?"

His eyes went wide as he sputtered, "N-no, b-but . . . ugh!" He pushed me back, striding toward the middle of the boat and plopping onto the floor. "This is stupid!"

I crouched beside him. "I know you don't believe me, but . . . trust me, please."

"Why should I?" he growled.

"Because I *really* don't like you, and I'm trying to help you anyway."

His eyes softened a little, and he was about to say something when Jonquil's booming voice interrupted. "How much longer will the boat hold, Fleck?"

I turned to see Jonquil on the floor with Scape, whose eyes were half-open.

"I think I can take it a bit farther," Fleck shouted

back to Jonquil. She was squinting, concentrating hard as she steered the sail.

In the darkness of the fog I could see the purple reflection in the orbs on Jonquil's and Scape's necks. They both had smoke necklaces.

Then I saw something else.

"We'll have to get to the graveyard before they figure out where we're going," Fleck continued.

"We'll never make it," Jonquil replied.

"Hey, you guys?" I tried to interrupt, pointing to the growing dark shape behind us. They ignored me.

"Well, what are we supposed to do? There will be guards all over the beach!"

"I think it's . . ." As I pointed, my finger shook.

"If we get caught by the soldiers," Fleck shouted, "then all five of us will be thrown into the Wall!"

"The Smoke Keeper!" I screamed, loud enough for everyone to hear. They all quieted and followed my finger, pointing into the fog.

Just visible in the distance was a large ship made from pitch-black wood. It was being carried through the air by rows and rows of Mireflies, tied to the ship with rope.

Just like in Jo's stories. Just like in my painting! But

these Mireflies weren't on fire, their black wings pumping up and down frantically.

The Smoke Keeper stood at the front of the vessel.

"What do we do?" I cried.

All of a sudden I felt dizzy. A loud hum filled my ears. I couldn't hear what everyone was shouting.

But the sky was growing brighter. I could see through the fog, as if something were illuminating us.

Then I remembered what it was.

I turned. The Wall rose behind us, impossibly tall, a swirl of glowing smoke.

"Turn! Turn!" Jonquil's shriek pierced through the hum, and I saw Fleck mouth back, "I can't."

We were heading straight for it. The Wall on one end and the Smoke Keeper closing in on us from the other.

Moments before we were about to crash, the boat creaked away, running alongside the Wall. But we were too close. I could feel my vision growing blurry and my head fuzzy.

Smoke Sick.

I turned back to see that Scape, Fleck, and Jonquil were all holding their breath, their cheeks puffed out. I did the same, then turned to Jeremiah—but he was nearly passed out already.

We have to wake up. We have to wake up now!

I went to grab the energy watch chain in Jeremiah's pocket, but it slid through my fingers, like it was just a hologram. I tried again, but it was the same.

What the heck? Is it because he has it in the real world?

"Rosemary! Hurry!"

I clamped my fingers over his nose. His eyes burst wide as he gasped for air. I covered his mouth to stop the smoke from getting in.

Wake up. Come on, wake up! I was pinching my arm over and over again, hoping it would send some signal to my body. *I have to wake up now.*

I looked up to see Fleck carving something into a bronze tile. Jonquil carried Scape on his back. He turned to me, uncovering his mouth and nose for only a moment to say, "Hurry, Rosemary! The boat's going to disappear!"

Seconds later a bronze bird, bigger than a motorcycle, soared out from the tile, hovering over the boat with squeaky flaps of its large wings.

I stood to follow the others as they climbed on its back, but then I heard Jeremiah cough, choking on the smoke. I rushed back to him.

What will happen if the Wall gets him? Will he really get hurt? Will he wake up?

"Stand up. Jeremiah, please stand up," I wheezed, taking the smallest breaths I could.

His eyelids fluttered, but he couldn't wake.

"Hurry, Rosemary! There's no time!"

I tried to lift him, but he was too heavy.

I can't leave him.

I knew that Jeremiah was cruel, and I knew that he didn't deserve my help. *Would he ever help me?* Of course not.

But I'm not like him, am I?

I waved the others forward, trying to tell them to go without me. I could barely hold my breath any longer.

I just had to keep us alive until we woke up, then we'd be fine. Everything would be fine.

"Well, hello, *children.*"

The voice sent a shiver down my spine.

I turned to see that Fleck, Scape, and Jonquil were gone—along with the big bronze bird. It was just me, Jeremiah, and the Smoke Keeper.

Thud. Thud. I felt the boat rock with footsteps as he strode off his ship onto ours.

As he walked toward me, he took a big breath in. I could see the smoke streaming into his mouth and nose. He smiled, then stood up taller—like he had grown even stronger. It was as if breathing in smoke was the same as breathing in air. Maybe for him it was.

"I'm going to throw both of you into the Wall," he growled, wrapping long, bony fingers around Jeremiah's ankle, "and then I'm going to drink you up—"

Before he could finish, the bronze bird rammed into him, throwing him backward onto his boat. He nearly flew off, into the Mire, but he snatched the edge of the ship just in time and pulled himself back in.

"Use your smoke, Rose!" I heard Fleck's faint voice as the bird flew back up into the air.

Jeremiah pushed himself backward, woozy.

Think, Rose, think. What would Jo do?

Well, of course, this was just like her competitions.

"What should I draw?" I would ask her.

"Whatever you need," she'd say.

I scrambled onto my knees, snatching up Fleck's nail that had dropped and rolled underneath the lip of the boat.

Then a white wooden block clattered to my feet.

I grabbed the block and scratched quickly. It was small, but maybe I could make it work.

I could hear the Smoke Keeper rise again, his joints cracking. "Mine. You're both mine."

As the smoke settled in my lungs, taking with it my ability to think, I found myself unable to worry. I just drew, like Jo had always told me.

I looked up to see the Smoke Keeper crawling across the ship. His bony arms and legs were fast and angular, like a spider's.

But my drawing was done. I watched it rise, glowing brown. Then it settled in my hand. It was a tiny wooden arrow, perfectly straight, and the curve of a bow. I snatched the elastic band from my hair. My brown curls fell free as I snapped the band to the bow.

I looked up, startled, to see the Smoke Keeper dragging a kicking Jeremiah onto the black ship.

Quickly, I dunked the tip of the arrow into the Mire, setting it ablaze. Then I fit it in the bow, as best as I could, and pulled back.

Twang.

The Smoke Keeper stopped for only a moment to watch the tiny arrow soar straight over his ship.

He grinned at me, toothy and wild. "It seems you missed, *girl*."

But I hadn't.

The arrow shot across the backs of a row of Mire-flies, lighting them on fire. The flames spread quickly down the ropes, to each Mirefly, and then slowly down the ship itself.

The Smoke Keeper's ship was on fire.

I did it! a proud little thought whispered.

"How dare you?" the Smoke Keeper's voice boomed out.

I expected him to retreat, but instead, he stormed across the boat, straight at me.

I was too frightened to move.

Then I noticed that the ground was glowing a faint purple.

The boat is going to explode. I need to wake up!

I didn't want to know what it would feel like to fall into the Mire, nor did I want to know what would happen if I was thrown into the Wall.

Right before either happened, however, Jeremiah pushed himself in front of me. The Smoke Keeper's bony fingers wrapped around his wrist instead of mine.

I was too shocked to think or try to stop it as the Smoke Keeper, in his rage, lifted Jeremiah and threw him. The moment he was in the air, it was as if the Wall were a vacuum sucking him in.

He made no sounds as he fell into the Wall. His eyes were wide, and his mouth was open. He was trapped, suspended in the middle of the swirling energy.

I wanted to scream, to say or do something, but I suddenly felt very weak. I could hear a ticking in my head.

"Now you," the Smoke Keeper said, the burning ship behind him.

But everything was turning gray. There was so much smoke, and it was everywhere. I could feel the floor of the boat giving out from under me.

The last thing I saw before I finally passed out was Jeremiah's face, trapped, frozen midscream inside the Wall.

I swear he was looking right at me.

THE WORLD OUTSIDE THE WATCH

Ugh."

I sat up quickly but regretted it. My whole body ached.

Why am I here? Why does everything hurt?

Then the memories streamed back: the slumber party, the battle with the Smoke Keeper, Jeremiah trapped in the Wall.

I glanced down at my body, but there were no bruises or burns. I would have expected some after last night. This must be the "phantom pain" Alejandro had told me about.

I felt my pockets, the ground, the cushions, but I couldn't find the watch. Jeremiah must have really taken it.

I'm the worst. Jo had given me only a couple of

rules, and I'd already broken the most important one.

There was only one way to fix it. I would have to find Jeremiah to get the watch back before he woke up.

I squinted at the old cat clock on the wall behind me. It was almost 10:00 a.m., and no one had come to wake me up.

At least it's Saturday, I thought, hurrying from the basement. I had to make this quick and then get out of there.

I snatched up my backpack and tiptoed up the stairs. I could smell eggs and waffles from the kitchen down the hall. *Must be Mr. and Mrs. Berg cooking breakfast.* They used to make us eggs and waffles after all our sleepovers.

I pushed the memory away and slid down a hall. Jeremiah's room was at the end, next to Fallon's. I really, really didn't want to wake anybody up. It'd be impossible to get the watch back if someone caught me now.

I pushed open Jeremiah's door.

The walls were covered in soccer posters. Jeremiah was still in bed, flat on his back.

He's still asleep, right? I'll have to be quiet.

I snuck up to his bedside, as silently as I could, but when I peered down, I wanted to scream. I slapped a hand over my mouth to stop myself.

His face was pale and drenched with sweat.

I stepped closer to inspect him. He took low, shallow breaths.

He wasn't dead, at least, but this was *really* weird.

I shook his shoulder and whispered his name, but it didn't work. I got bolder, louder, rougher, but still he lay there.

What if he couldn't wake up because he was trapped in the Wall? Alejandro thought that our minds could enter alternate realities but not our bodies, right? Then what if Jeremiah's mind had gotten stuck there?

Will he be like this forever?

All at once I felt panicked. I had to do something. I had to help him.

I ripped the covers off and saw the watch in his fist.

I pried it from his warm fingers, dropped it back into my pocket, and replaced his blanket.

If he was trapped in the dreamworld, it was probably my job to get him out.

I clicked Jeremiah's door shut behind me, then stopped to listen outside Fallon's room. I wanted to know if all the girls were awake yet.

I pressed an ear to the door and listened. I could hear the soft sounds of someone snoring.

Good. It's still safe.

"Oh! Rosemary, dear! You're awake!" I spun around to see Mrs. Berg wearing an apron. She was smiling. I suddenly felt very bad about Jeremiah. What would she think when she saw him? I couldn't tell her the truth. She wouldn't believe me.

"I was coming to get you kids for breakfast!"

"Everyone's still asleep," I mumbled, my eyes down. I couldn't face her.

"Oh, all right. Then I guess we can wait." She suddenly gasped. "Rosemary!"

I looked up quickly, aware that my heart was beating much faster than it should.

"What?"

"Your face!"

I turned to see my reflection in a portrait on the wall.

I expected maybe bruises from last night, but instead, there were thick black and red Sharpie lines.

Someone had drawn a mustache on me, connected my eyebrows, drawn spots all over my face. "GROSSY" was written in big letters across my forehead. I couldn't stop the blush from reaching to the tops of my ears.

They must have done it while I was asleep. I guess that's when Jeremiah stole my watch.

"Who did that?" Mrs. Berg whispered with concern, her hand around my cheek so that she could get a better look.

"It's nothing," I said, pulling my face away. "It was just a game," I muttered, pushing past her.

"Oh." I turned back to see her eyes screwed up in pity. It was like she knew I was lying. "Well, let me help you wash it off, and then you can get some breakfast. How does that sound?" she asked, her big smile returning.

I shook my head. "I kind of want to go home. Do you mind if I call my mom and wait outside?"

I really didn't want to run into any of the girls when they started waking up.

"That's fine, hon."

Mom can't see me like this. It'll break her heart.

"Actually, yeah, could you please help me wash this off first?"

"Sooo, how was the party?" Mom sang.

For a second I thought about telling her what had really happened. Telling her that it had been a bad idea for me to go in the first place and that I never wanted to do it again . . . but then she smiled at me.

If I told her, then she'd just get sad again. I didn't want to disappoint her.

Instead, I said, "Good. It was fun."

"Right? I knew it would be! You just have to give things a chance, my love!"

THE BOOK

As soon as we got home, I rushed to my room and locked the door. I needed a plan of action.

Maybe Jeremiah *would* wake up on his own. Then all I'd have to do was convince him that neither the Wall nor the watch was real.

If he didn't wake up, that was a lot scarier. I would have to find a way to get him out of the Wall before he died . . . or, at least, before his mind did.

My stomach hurt just thinking about it.

A plan, I need a plan, I thought as I paced.

"If you want to win, you need a plan," Jo's voice echoed in my memory.

Jo had told me so many stories, but I guess I hadn't paid enough attention—I didn't know the stories could possibly be real, so I didn't realize how important all the details were.

And now Jo was gone. I couldn't ask her questions about what to do or where to go.

Why didn't she give me specific instructions or something?

I stopped pacing, a realization holding me still. *But what if she* did *leave instructions?*

I rushed to my closet. Up on the highest shelf, tucked away in the back, was a dusty old book—the storybook about the clock world. What if it wasn't just a storybook after all? What if it was a guide?

I held it as gently as I could, afraid that somehow, after years of sitting there, it might fall apart at my touch.

I blew the dust off the worn cover. Over the years the red leather had faded to more of a brick brown, and the once-gold threading was tinged with age too, save for in the middle of the braids where some luminous gold still winked out.

The Thirteenth Hour.

It looked the same as it had in my memories. This book felt more different and special than any other. It always had.

It had been a long time since I'd looked at this book,

and I wondered how much I'd forgotten. One page, however, stuck out. I flipped to it, near the back.

Amisi was flying over a city where everyone wore masks and rode on giant turtles. An electric-blue dragon soared alongside Amisi—it glowed the same shade of brown as the things I had drawn in Eleven.

The inscription read: *Amisi found himself at the Eleventh Hour, where everyone danced. The people of Eleven were so happy because they could create anything using only a pen and their imagination.*

It really was the world I had discovered in my dreams, and it had been here all along.

I went back a handful of pages to see a farm, but instead of a farmhouse, there was a huge matchbox, and in place of a windmill was a rainbow-colored pinwheel. Surrounding the strange scene were whole fields of apple trees that only came up to a farmer's knees—I couldn't tell if they were tiny or if he was a giant.

The man held a red apple in the palm of his hand. It was surrounded by glowing red energy that swirled like a tornado.

It reminded me of how Fleck's purple smoke moved.

I guess the red of Six and the blue of Eleven combined into purple—makes sense.

Amisi found himself at the Sixth Hour, the text

read, *where nothing was the size it was supposed to be—because the farmers of Six could make anything bigger or smaller, even themselves!*

So this is Fleck's world, I thought, *or half her world, at least.* I stared intently at the farmer, satisfied by the spray of freckles spattered across his cheeks.

I reached over my desk and grabbed a Post-it Note. I scribbled, *Six, Fleck.* Then I stuck the Post-it in the corner of the farmer's page.

I figured Jo hadn't collected the energy from Six, because I didn't see red Smoke in the watch when I was in Eleven. I put an *X* on the Post-it.

One down, eleven worlds to go.

Jonquil's smoke was a very light blue, which meant he was the blue of Eleven and the white of Three, represented in the book's drawing by a dark mountain that *floated* above the ground, a black ocean underneath. A woman with long yellow hair was just visible, lofting her hand above her head, shooting white smoke and fire toward the mountain.

I put a Post-it with a check mark on it on that page. There was white smoke in the watch, I realized with relief. I didn't want to have to go to the scary fire mountain.

Then there was Scape's green smoke. I matched it to

a page that looked straight out of a cartoon—the people there had yellow smoke, it seemed. A man had presumably been run over by a wild carriage, his body perfectly flat on the ground. But what was strange was that he had peeled his head up off the ground to look at the carriage as it pulled away. His whole body was awash with a sunny yellow glow.

That page's sticky note got a check mark too.

I got excited—maybe my plan would work. All I had to do was find out which other worlds Jo had already gotten smoke from. After that, I could figure out how to get smoke from the rest.

I found the last three colors of smoke that were in the watch. The bright violet smoke was from Nine, where everything was covered in snow. The black smoke was from Two, where a boy sailed straight *into* the sky. And, last, the pink energy came from Eight, where the people tunneled underground.

By the time I had found all of the colors, the book was covered in Post-its. There were seven kinds of smoke I needed to collect, including Eleven's.

No wonder Jo never got it—the Smoke Keeper of Eleven was terrifying. How was I supposed to steal smoke from him when he had his guards around all the time?

And how was I going to get smoke from the Smoke Keepers, anyway? Plug their noses and ask them to sneeze? I doubted the Smoke Keepers from the other worlds would be any nicer than the one from Eleven.

I wished Jo were around so I could talk to her, ask her what I should do.

"Just buck up and save that brat's life!" is probably what she'd say. I giggled at the thought, but then the nerves crept back in.

I shouldn't be in charge of someone living or dying. There shouldn't be any worlds inside watches. Jo shouldn't be missing.

I read through the book again and again, trying to find clues on how I was going to survive in these odd places.

But there was something strange, I realized. There should be twelve worlds, but there were only eleven.

My fingers slid over the bumpy-but-soft surface of the thick paper, counting. Where Twelve should be was nothing. The book just . . . ended.

Where was Twelve?

I pulled out the watch, just to make sure there even was a twelve on it. I clicked the button. The petals fell open, revealing the glistening face inside.

I held the open watch up to my face; the petals were

so close that I could see the tiniest etchings in the bright flowers of Ten.

One. Two. Three. Four. Five. Six. As I held the watch, I wondered if I was holding many worlds and all of their people in my palm. *Seven. Eight. Nine. Ten. Eleven.*

But twelve wasn't there. That was the petal that had gone missing.

I closed my eyes and tried to remember what it had looked like. When Jo had shown it to me when I was little . . . what had been there?

The image was fuzzy, but I seemed to faintly recall a perfect place. With perfect clouds, tiny perfect people. They all surrounded what looked like a fairy-tale castle.

I wonder why it isn't in the book?

I added a final Post-it to the bottom of Eleven's page: *Twelve: Fairy-tale castle?*

I guess I was going to have to leave that one until last. Maybe I could learn about it in the other worlds.

I continued reading, studying.

My favorite page was the one with a girl who sat on a swing that was carried into the air by bronze-colored bubbles. *Amisi found himself at One,* I read, *whose Princess likes riddles and puzzles, but hates fun and losing. When she's happy, she's down, and when she's sad, she's up.*

I also liked the picture of giant stone faces with tiny legs poking out the bottom. *Amisi found himself at Five,* it said, *whose people hide in stone heads and run around bashing into each other for fun.*

Finally, I flipped to the last page. There were two men silhouetted inside ornate, oval frames. The man on top was the thin man with the floppy mustache, Amisi. He smiled and looked bright and kind.

Under his portrait was his name: *Olaf Amisi – Author.*

Then just below was a second man. He was squarer than Amisi, his face all hard angles and clean lines, a flop of tawny hair swooping over his brow as if it were wrapped like a present. He didn't look bright, and he certainly didn't look kind.

He did—I realized, my belly sinking—look quite a bit like Wes. As if confirming my suspicion, underneath the man's face was a name: *Harold Marks – Illustrator.*

I gasped. When I was little, I hadn't been able to read cursive. I never realized what this page said. I didn't understand that the person who made this book might be related to me.

Maybe Jo had gotten the watch from him. Maybe he had been to Eleven and had drawn the ghostly pictures because he was an artist too.

Like me.

The thought made me smile.

Maybe I *could* do this. I could collect all of the smoke, destroy the Wall, and save Jeremiah. The magical world was in my blood.

I hid the book back in my closet and flopped onto my bed.

I felt like I should start now. I checked my watch. It was 2:00. I didn't need to go to Two. Plus, I wasn't even sleepy.

Maybe I can get sleepy by five o'clock if I go for a bike ride, and then drink a glass of warm milk, and then do my math homework, and then—

My train of thought was interrupted when Mom popped her head in my room. She was smiling so widely that I got suspicious.

"Your friend is here!"

"My what?"

Who could it be?

Wait. Alejandro's shaggy head popped up in my memory. *Could he have found my house . . . ?*

"Fallon."

"*What?*"

I shot up, smoothing my hair back. Why would she come to see me?

"Maybe I left something at her house?" I said aloud, hurrying to the front door.

Sure enough, Fallon was standing on the other side. Her bright green bike was leaning against her leg. She didn't look up at me.

"Hey, Fallon, what's up?" I asked, trying to pretend this whole thing wasn't super weird.

"Mom wanted you to have your goody bag," she mumbled, shoving a clear plastic bag forward. Inside I could see a bottle of sparkly nail polish, a Hyung-Gyun bracelet, and candy.

"Thanks," I replied, feeling even more awkward. *She really came all the way to give me this?*

There was a pause. My fingers tapped on the doorknob. I didn't know what to do.

"Do you need anything else?" I asked, unable to take the silence anymore.

She finally looked up at me, her eyes watery.

"D-did you notice anything weird about Jer?"

My heartbeat sped up, and I could feel sweat beading on my forehead. "What do you mean?"

"He"—she hiccupped, trying to hold her emotions in—"he didn't wake up this morning."

He's in the Wall, I wanted to scream. *It's my fault. I'll fix it.* But instead, I stood numb, staring like a fish.

"He what?"

Tears were falling freely down her face now. "He j-just didn't wake up. They d-don't know why. We took him to the hospital, b-but they don't know—"

I hadn't seen Fallon cry in so long. She used to cry a lot, and I'd always been there for her. Not Jeremiah or Samantha Plank. She always came to me. And every time I saw her crying, it hurt me too.

Without thinking, I stepped outside and put an arm around her, patting her back while she quietly hiccuped the tears back in.

"It'll be okay," I said.

"B-but what if he doesn't wake up again?"

"He will." *I promise.*

"I—I didn't know who to tell. Mom and Dad are s-so scared about everything, and I . . ." She trailed off, sniffing, then pushed herself away from me, wiping her eyes. "I was just wondering if you noticed anything different about him."

His wide-open mouth and shocked eyes, staring at me from the Wall.

"I don't think so," I whispered.

She nodded, wiping the rest of her tears away with a swipe of her sleeve.

"I figured not. Oh well."

She turned to go, her bike wheels squeaking. Then she turned back, her eyes were on the ground again.

"I'm sorry."

"For what?"

But she didn't answer. She just hopped on the bike and pedaled away.

I shut the door, reeling. I had been waiting for Fallon to say that for a long, long time, but the only thing I could focus on was the fact that Jeremiah really wasn't going to wake up.

That meant I definitely had to destroy that Wall.

"What was that?" Mom asked, wandering over with a big smile and her hands on her hips. "Ooh! Cute goody bag!"

"She came over to tell me . . ." I paused, thinking.

"Tell you what?"

"You know her brother, Jeremiah?"

"Yeah?"

"He didn't wake up this morning."

Mom called the Bergs, thinking maybe with her nursing knowledge she could offer something or help somehow. It sounded like they all thought this was some weird fluke. The hospital was running tests.

Aside from being comatose, nothing else seemed to be wrong with Jeremiah.

I felt awful the rest of the day. If only I had saved him in those last few moments, he would be all right.

I mean, he wouldn't be *all right*, I guess. He'd still be a huge jerk . . . but at least he'd be an awake jerk. And Fallon and the Bergs wouldn't cry.

That night I lay in bed seriously debating if I should keep the watch on me.

I was scared, to be honest, to go back into the clock world. Maybe it was better if I didn't return if this was the kind of trouble I was going to cause.

But then I couldn't get Fallon's red, teary eyes out of my head.

I had to destroy the Wall to save Jeremiah, and I had only five days to do it, based on what Scape had said the day I'd met them. I had to find all the Smoke Keepers and steal their smoke.

Impossible, a small voice in my head said.

I clicked the watch open. It was 1:15 a.m. I'd been far too jittery to even attempt sleeping a few hours ago at 10:00, but now . . .

I stared at the first petal, thought of the picture in the book of the girl on her swing. *The Princess,* I thought.

If the Kings and Queens were the Smoke Keepers, then she'd be related to them, right? Was she even still alive? The book was written so long ago.

That world, One, didn't seem so scary. It looked light and bubbly and fun. Yes, that would be a good place to start.

The hands of the watch spun as I thought about it, lulling me to sleep.

I hoped the Princess was alive, I decided. I wanted to meet her.

ONE

I woke into nothingness—not knowing if I was right-side, wrong-side, up-side, or down-side. My head felt silly too. My body was light. I wasn't tired at all.

"Hiddly, piddly, widdly, woo, she was a poor one, Little Girl Blue."

I sat up at the strange sound. The voice was quiet and loud at the same time. Far away but high and piercing. *It's a girl,* I thought, but my mind was so full of fuzz that I couldn't think much beyond that.

"Hiddly, piddly, widdly, wink, the sad little girl fell in the sink."

As the singing continued, I stood. All around me was fog, wafting like steam from a warm mug of cocoa. The ground was so soft that I felt no resistance as I walked, like I was going to fall with every step—as if I were just walking on clouds. It took me a moment to get used to the sensation.

I followed the voice.

"Hiddly, piddly, widdly, woe, no one knew where it might go."

The fog opened onto a clearing of what seemed to be very thin trees. But when I tried to touch the bark of one with my hand, it evaporated; it was just an illusion. The way the sun sparkled through the fog, bleeding through it like a drop of paint in a glass of water, looked like an illusion too.

"Hiddly, piddly, widdly, when, her mother never found her again."

Then I turned and there she was.

The girl was younger than me, with a fluffy halo of tightly curled black hair. Her eyes were wide saucers of bronze, and she wore a heavy coat that looked like it was made of massive cotton balls. As I drew nearer, able now to hear the soft lull of her hum, I noticed she wasn't standing but sitting, and yet we were eye to eye.

I peered into the cover of gray and found that she was sitting on a plain plank of driftwood. Strings shot up from every end of it and connected to a cloud of sparkling bubbles above her.

Nestled in her curls, I caught the glint of a crown.

She's the Princess, I realized with a start. *The Princess from One.*

"Wowie wow, and who are you?"

She was looking into me in a way that made me think she could see my bones.

"I'm . . . Rosemary."

She laughed, though I don't know why. "Strange name, strange girl."

She held a strange bottle. It was large and bulbous and round, like a fishbowl—only instead of fish, it was filled with a luminous, iridescent liquid that rolled over itself, slick like oil.

The Princess dipped a large metal circle into the liquid, then held it above her head and blew. Bronze smoke filled the ring and made a flurry of bubbles that shot up, joining the cloud that held her aloft.

It's just like in the picture.

That meant that I had made it to my intended destination, but I would have to work fast. I needed to find the Smoke Keeper of this world and steal its smoke.

It can't possibly be this odd little girl, I decided. She seemed too nice.

"I actually came to, uh, well, ask you for help," I shouted up at her.

Her driftwood swing rocked from side to side. As she moved, she began to glow bronze.

She rocked slowly at first, but then arced wider and wider until she was upside down. She stopped there, the bubbles at my feet and her toes above my head. Still, the bubbles didn't pop or rise, the swing didn't fall, and the Princess looked like this all was quite normal. She blew more bubbles that then shot to the ground below.

Or was it above?

The more I stared at the upside-down girl, the less certain I was of which one of us was right-side-up.

"Play with me," she cried, rocking her swing again until it was upright. "If you win my game, I will give you one present," her voice tinkled.

"Okay," I said. I did need help, and I didn't know how else I was going to find the Smoke Keeper. "What do you want me to play?"

She laughed, clapping her small hands. "Tell me what I like, and don't tell me what I don't. If you figure out *why* I like what I like, then my feet will touch the ground and you will win. If I float out of sight, then you lose."

"I don't know what that means," I said. *A riddle?*

"Then I won't help you." She blew a gust of bubbles, and her swing rose. "Goodbye." As she drifted higher and higher, I lost sight of her in the fog.

"Wait!" I shouted, hoping to bring her back. "I'll play!"

"Then what do I like?" her little voice chimed from the air.

I tried to remember what I'd read about this strange girl in the book.

The Princess likes riddles and puzzles, but hates fun and losing. When she's happy, she's down, and when she's sad, she's up.

"Do you like a . . . ," I began, still uncertain of how this could possibly be correct, "puzzle?"

"I do like puzzles!" she shrieked from above me. I watched as she slowly fell.

"Do you like a . . . riddle?"

"Yes, yes I do!" She fell closer still.

"But you don't like boring things?"

"Ugh." And she floated higher, out of sight again.

"Wait—I said you *don't* like them, though!"

"Tell me what I like, and don't tell me what I don't," she repeated, sounding a bit angry now.

"Do you like . . ." I had to think very hard. If I messed this up, then she'd be so far above me that I wouldn't be able to hear her anymore. I couldn't lose. "Bubbles?"

After a frightening pause her feet dangled lower.

"I like bubbles."

We played for ages, it seemed, her little swing floating up or drifting down, until my throat was anxious and tight.

"Cake?" *Everyone likes cake, right?*

"No, no, no!" She floated higher again.

"Do you like a puppy?"

"Oh, yes!"

"A kitten, then!"

"Certainly!"

Ah! She was getting close now, and if I could only get her down a few more feet, then her feet might touch the ground. "So then, you like dogs, too!"

All I got that time was a laugh before she shot up.

"How can you like puppies but not dogs? It doesn't make any sense!"

"Play my game."

"It's not a game, it's nonsense!"

But what if it isn't nonsense? Jo often played silly games with me, but there were always rules—even if they didn't make sense at first.

For the first time in what seemed like an endless string of random guessing, I thought I might be getting somewhere.

Okay . . . so she liked puppies, but not dogs, sheep, but not cows. She liked the Queen, beef, grass, and jazz.

She didn't like floating, flowers, presents, or candies.

And she liked a riddle, but not questions.

But what's the common denominator?

"Do you like . . ." I thought about all the words. *Ooh, maybe she only likes things that are a certain number of letters!* I'd start small. "Do you like pie?"

"No, why?" She giggled as she rose higher.

What else, what else? I had nothing. Maybe she only likes when there's one of something instead of multiple things?

"Do you like a good book?"

"I love a good book!" *Yes! She's coming back down.*

"What about a box, a toy, a bow?"

"No, no, no!" She rose higher and faster than before. What had I done? I was never going to win now. *Think, Rose, think* . . . Jo had always told me that if I got stuck on a problem, I should draw it out.

I kneeled on the ground, picked up a pointy stone, and wrote out all the words I could remember asking her in two columns in the cloudy dirt—the yes column and the no column.

"Bubbles and riddles over here, but dogs and losing over—"

Wait a minute! Now that I had written it out, I could see the answer to this riddle.

"I know . . . do you like being silly?"

She bounced in her seat. "I do!"

"And kitties?"

"I love kitties!"

She was falling to the ground faster and faster.

"And noodles?"

"Yes!"

"Okay . . . then what about me? A buddy?"

"I like buddies," she declared just as her bare toes hung inches from the ground.

"I knew it!"

"Then what is it I like?"

"You like double letters, don't you?"

"Clever, clever, clever!" She hopped off the swing, dancing a circle around me in the mist. The path of her hands glowed a soft bronze in the fog, sparkling faintly.

"Now it's time for your prize! I'll take you all the way up to my castle!" She pointed directly above us. I had to crane my neck to see. But if I looked hard and squinted, I could just make out the twinkling lights of a city above.

"Actually," I said, crossing my fingers in my pockets, "I was hoping that you might be able to do me a different favor."

"Oh?"

"I want," I said, debating what to ask, "I want you to bring me to the Smoke Keeper."

"It's done."

"What? Where?"

She smiled . . . revealing long, cracked, yellow teeth.

A shriek caught in my throat.

"What do you want from me, buddy?" she asked, her voice sounding much scarier now than it had before. "Let me see you."

Then she grabbed her large bronze eyes, pulling them right out of her head. I realized, looking through the fog, that what I'd thought were her eyes were only bubbles. She released them, revealing dark caverns where her eyes had been.

I scrambled back, unable to speak, already lost in the fog.

"What's wrong, buddy? Why were you looking for me?"

I tried to run, but it was too hard on the cloudy ground. *I have to go faster.*

I stopped to draw a race car in the dirt, but nothing happened.

My powers in Eleven don't work here. But Fleck said I could use all the powers—maybe I can float like the girl? Isn't that the power here?

"Why don't you show me your smoke, buddy? What are you trying to hide?"

I scampered behind one of the tall trees as I tried to remember how the Princess—no, the Smoke Keeper— had made her bubbles.

She just blew, didn't she?

As quietly as I could, I tried to blow out. To my amazement, a flood of smoke followed, creating a cloud that floated away.

I didn't have any bubble liquid like she did, but maybe I could still find a way.

I kneeled on the ground and blew a new cloud of smoke, then I stepped on it.

"Whoa." It was wobbly, but I was rising.

Now what? How am I going to get the Smoke Keeper's smoke?

"Your smoke looks strange. Why does it look strange?"

I looked up to find the Smoke Keeper hanging upside down right above me.

"You're not from around here, are you?" she hissed, pushing me off my smoke cloud. I screamed as I plummeted.

Seconds before I hit the ground, she caught my wrist.

"You're *naughty*, not a buddy."

I could feel her long nails digging into my skin.

"I will take you to the Wall, naughty girl."

I flailed. I had to get away. If Jeremiah and I both got trapped in the clock world, then no one would be able to save us.

In a last-ditch effort I threw my body up and managed to clamber onto the swing behind her.

She howled, trying to throw me off.

I reached for something, anything, to keep me up, but all I could grab was one of her bubbles.

I fell backward and hit the ground hard.

"Ow."

I felt very dizzy. *I have to get her smoke. How do I get her—*

"Clumsy, wumsy Rosey," she sang. "Where did you goesy?"

She was getting closer.

SHHK.

The sound reverberated in my head. I was feeling dizzier. This wasn't just from the fall, it was how I felt before I was about to wake up in the real world.

But I have to get smoke before I go back.

I looked at the bubble. Bronze smoke swirled inside.

I wonder . . .

"Rosey, Posey, Wosey? Where are you hiding?"

Whoosh. A loud sound filled the landscape. *Someone's waking me up.*

I pulled out the watch—relieved to see it was a Smoke Ball in this world as well—and held the bubble in front of it. I squeezed hard, popping the magic bubble. Smoke poured out—and was sucked straight into the glowing energy of the watch.

I did it!

"There you are! I found you," the Smoke Keeper said. Then she gasped. "What is that—"

Whoosh.

I screamed as the creature's face zoomed right in front of me. I could feel her hand on mine, struggling for the Smoke Ball.

"No!"

WHOOSH.

THE PLAN

R osey! Wake up!"

Whoosh, whoosh, whoosh. The blankets rustled as my mother shook my shoulder.

"Mom?" My voice was hoarse. I sat up, rubbing my eyes. My room was so bright compared to the foggy forest of One.

"You were having a nightmare, bubala." Mom's eyes were wide.

Suddenly, I felt very awake.

"How do you know?"

"You were screaming."

I was screaming in the real world too?

"Like *screaming* screaming?" I asked.

"Well, quietly," Mom said. "But it was screaming. You were muttering about something too."

"What did I say?" I asked, afraid of the answer.

"Oh, you said 'ow' and something about smoke." Mom waved her hand. "What were you dreaming about?"

I thought about the Princess and her horrible, long teeth.

"I don't know," I muttered.

"Sheesh, with that kind of screaming, I thought for sure you'd remember." She ran a hand through my hair. "Sure you're feeling all right?"

I nodded, aware of how sweaty my hair and blankets were. It had been a scary dream, so scary that I thought about it all day. Maybe I only thought about it because I couldn't bear to think about Jo.

Everything was scary. Everything was going wrong. If she were here, it would all be okay.

When night came, I didn't dare sleep again—long teeth filling my memory.

I stayed up all night, and when Mom came to wake me up in the morning, I was already dressed for school.

I trudged out of the Dino-Wagon feeling like a zombie, my feet made of lead.

I must have looked silly, dragging my feet through the grass, because people were staring. *Whatever. Let them think what they want. It's not like they have to worry about a boy trapped in an evil wall that's draining the life out of him like he's a Capri Sun, thank you very much.*

And, of course, who was standing there right by the front doors of the school? None other than Samantha Plank and her posse. She was wearing lip gloss today. Whenever she wore lip gloss, she always had little bits of hair and other things trapped in it. She snarled a shiny lip at me as I passed by—apparently too close for her liking. Under her breath I heard the "ew" she muttered to her friends.

"Must be nice to only have to worry about how many dead bugs are stuck to your lips." The stress must have been getting to me because I really hadn't meant to say that out loud.

I pushed down an evil smile when Samantha gasped and her friends giggled. Maybe I should say things out loud more often.

Class was just as boring as usual. In history Mrs. Lee was talking about the Crimean War. It was hard to focus, however, because there was a war going on *right now* in the watch in my pocket.

I looked around. Everyone was boring.

The real world felt so gray compared to the watch world. I found myself itching to take a nap, to slip into a place that was different, where *I* was different.

Plus, I'd already wasted one day—I only had until Wednesday to save Jeremiah.

"If you want to win, you need a plan." It was like the memory of Jo was mocking me.

Fine, all right, I'll make a plan.

I had six worlds left and little more than two days. That meant I'd have to fall asleep, like, three times a day! I didn't even know if that was possible.

Maybe I could . . . , I started thinking, scribbling on my notepad, *set my alarm every hour? Then I could knock out Five, Six, and Seven. . . . But what if I haven't collected the smoke within the hour? Then my alarm would wake me up and a whole other half day would be lost.*

So maybe I can signal someone outside the world to wake me up. Mom heard me when I talked, right? Yeah, I'll just have to do that.

I tapped my pencil, lost in thought. This was hard. Aside from Five, Six, and Seven, I also had to get smoke from Ten, Eleven, and the unknown Twelve.

I didn't want to go back to Eleven until I had all the rest, though. It would be a wasted trip. Plus, that Smoke

Keeper scared me the most. He had already seen me. He knew I wasn't supposed to be there, and he would try to throw me into the Wall the second he saw me again.

I would have only one shot to steal his smoke, and I wasn't ready yet.

Then maybe—I picked up my pencil, jotting my thoughts in my journal once again—*I could go to Ten tonight, Twelve tomorrow night, and Eleven on Wednesday morning.*

I'd have to work really, really fast, though. If I was too slow, then, poof, Jeremiah would be gone forever.

And what about Five, Six, and Seven?

The pressure started to overwhelm me.

This wasn't a game or a riddle, it was reality. I had only the rest of today, tomorrow, and part of the next day to save someone's life.

My breathing got faster, and my chest felt tight. *What if I can't do it?* I put a hand to my chest, feeling my heartbeat. I was sweating again. I was panicking. *It's too many worlds—*

"Psst."

I spun around. Alejandro was behind me, sharpening his pencil at the counter. Today he wore a tie-dyed shirt that said BYTE ME on it.

"You feeling okay?" he whispered.

I nodded, realizing how strange I must have looked breathing so hard and clutching at my chest.

I looked around; others were staring at me too.

"You sure? You look pale—"

"Ms. Marks and Mr. Fuentes! Do you have something you'd like to share with the class?" Mrs. Lee barked.

"No, ma'am. Just asking Rosemary if I could borrow a pencil."

As Alejandro answered, I scribbled a note on a scrap of paper: *Lunch? Need your help.*

Mrs. Lee raised her eyebrows. "Aren't you sharpening a pencil as we speak?"

Alejandro looked down at his now-sharp pencil as if surprised.

"Oh! Look at that! I forgot." The class giggled. I heard Samantha whisper, "Dummy," to Jackson sitting beside her, but Alejandro didn't seem to care. He walked back to his desk, and as he passed me, I slipped him the note.

I saw him unfold it at his seat, then he looked back at me with a smile and a thumbs-up. I smiled back. Maybe, just maybe, if I had help, I could save Jeremiah after all.

I tried to listen to the lesson after that, I really tried, but it was impossible with the watch in my pocket. Nothing else seemed important. Instead, I listened to another piece of Jo's advice: *"If you're not sure what to do, draw it out."*

So I drew. I drew everything I knew about Five, Six, and Seven in my notebook.

I drew a big stone head from Five, surrounding it with sandy smoke. I drew what I thought the person inside the big stone head might look like, with spindly little legs.

I drew the farmer holding his giant apple in Six and the matchbox farmhouse behind him. I wondered if all the people in *The Thirteenth Hour* were the Smoke Keepers, as the girl on the swing had been. This farmer looked so nice, though, like a grandfather. I couldn't believe he was a monster.

Then again, the cute little Princess was.

Then I drew the woman in Seven, who was covered from head to toe in metal: jewelry, pots and pans, door-knobs. They were all stuck to her. The book had said she could attract metal like a magnet. I could only just barely see her face through the mass of gold, bronze, and iron—a silvery smoke making everything glow.

Just as I finished a diagram of the massive metal building behind the woman, the bell rang.

I tossed my notebook in my backpack and stood to leave when Mrs. Lee raised her hands.

"One moment, students. One moment, please." The class groaned, sitting back down.

"I have an unfortunate announcement I'd like to make." Now everyone went quiet. "You may have noticed that our dear Jeremiah and Fallon are out today."

I looked up. I hadn't even noticed that Fallon's chair was empty too.

"I have been informed that Jeremiah will be out sick for some time. Tomorrow I think we ought to spend some time writing him get-well cards, yes?"

The class nodded along, still quiet.

"All right, now you may go."

And then everyone stood all at once, a chorus of voices filling the room. I couldn't hear what anyone was saying, but I figured they were talking about what had happened to Jeremiah.

If only you knew, I thought.

Alejandro and I met in the church at lunchtime. I couldn't tell him about the watch. (Rule #1.) Instead, I asked him, "So do you really want to make a game together?"

"Absolutely!" he said a little too loudly, his voice echoing up the steeple of the church. "What do you want to make?"

I laughed, nervous, before pulling out my notebook. "Funny you should ask. I have an idea, actually, but I need your help in figuring out the, uh, *gameplay*."

I told him that in this game we'd travel among worlds with different powers. "But I don't know how to beat the bosses of them, see—"

"I can help!" he interjected, spilling his chocolate milk.

I showed him the pictures I'd drawn and explained everything I could about Five, Six, and Seven.

"And all I have to do as the player is get the bosses to release their magic out of their ears?" he asked.

"Or get them to use enough of it that you can steal some. It looks like a cloud, I think, when they use a lot of magic."

"Hmm. A cloud will be tough in terms of the graphics, but for the farmer guy I would probably find, like, a big wheat stalk, then I'd make it really big so that I could tickle his nose from far away until he sneezed. Boom. Magic everywhere!"

I winced, imagining how gross a Smoke Keeper's sneeze would be, but I nodded along, writing Alejandro's idea down in my notepad. "Good, good."

"For the metal lady I think I'd just keep throwing metal at her, since she automatically attracts it, and it'd eventually smack her in the face. At some point she'd have to exhale a big cloud of magic."

That's not a bad idea. I'd just have to find enough metal.

"And what's the deal with this strong-looking dude?" he asked, picking up the drawing of Five. "Is the big stone face hollow? Or is the guy flattened underneath it? Or is the rock face his actual face?"

"Uh . . ." I tapped my pencil, trying to remember what I could from the book. "I'm not sure?"

"Well, in that case, there's only one thing to do to a face."

"What's that?"

He shrugged. "Punch it really hard until it explodes."

Ah. I shivered. That . . . was not something I wanted to try.

"Where did you get these ideas, anyway?" he asked, looking at the drawings closely. "They look so real."

"Yeah, well, um, I dream them up mostly. When I'm sleeping."

"That's really cool! I wish I could do that." Alejandro's face fell. "I don't actually have dreams I can remember." He perked up a moment later. "Anyway, when do you want to start creating the game?"

"I was actually wondering if we could meet here again at five?"

"Five a.m. or five p.m.?" he responded. Before I could ask who the heck is up at 5:00 in the morning, he continued, "Because I'm free at five a.m. tomorrow, but I have a Future Coders Club meeting from four to six p.m."

"Wait, what? You're actually up at five a.m.?"

"Yeah, my mom drops me off really early every morning on her way to work. I've been coming here and doing homework and playing games and stuff before school starts. But you're free to join me!"

I grimaced. I didn't think I'd ever gotten up that early, but then I remembered what would happen if I didn't have someone to wake me while I hopped hours.

Only a few days left to save Jeremiah . . .

"Let's do it."

THE INVITATION

That night I ate my grilled cheese in three bites. I did my homework, all of it, even the essay we were assigned, in one hour. I convinced Mom that it was a good idea to take me to school at 5:00 a.m. so that I could join the Game Development Club. Then I sat in front of Mom's laptop, watching every action movie compilation I could find for inspiration.

After all the planning I did at school, it felt like a switch had been flipped and my blood started running hotter. I was prepared for anything.

"Rosemary? Are you here?"

Except for that.

I dropped the broom handle I was using to mimic a fighting pose in *Rambo III* and poked my head out my bedroom door. "Dad?" I called, stepping into the hall.

What was he doing here? He had never come to Mom's house before.

An excited thought popped into my mind: *Maybe he's found Jo.*

I hurried into the living room. Jo would help me save Jeremiah—she'd know exactly what to do.

But the second I saw my parents on the couch, their faces drawn and gray, I knew it wasn't good news.

"Oh, Rosemary!" Wes launched up, taking big strides to me. I backed away—but then he hugged me. I didn't know what to do with my arms. My dad never hugged.

"We still haven't found her," he said, letting go. "I've run out of ideas."

I glanced over his shoulder at Mom, who shrugged, obviously as weirded out by Dad's unusually messy appearance as I was. Normally, his hair was slicked back perfectly, and his suits were pressed. He was wearing sweatpants, for crying out loud. I had never seen Wes Marks go outside wearing something without buttons before!

"But I do have some good news," he said, guiding me back to the couch. "I managed to get footage showing that Joanne sent a letter from the postbox outside the hospital the day she disappeared. You didn't happen to get anything, did you?"

I shook my head. *I wish.* It was good to know that Jo was still out there somewhere, though.

"Oh, well, I'd just hoped." His face looked sad again. He looked tired, too. "I drove around the city today, visited all of her old hangouts—no one has seen her. I'll drive around Globe tomorrow."

He peered up at me, uncertain. "Do you want to come with me? Look for her together?"

My eyes went wide. I'd never expect my father to ask to spend time with me when he didn't have to. What was going on?

He took my small hand in both of his big ones. His hands were soft. I hadn't expected that, either.

"I was hard on Joanne because I wanted her to be happy. But when she didn't want to see me in the hospital and then just disappeared without a word, I realized"— he paused, sighing—"I realized maybe I made a mistake. I think I've made a number of mistakes."

I had no idea what to say. To see Wes acting so . . . warm and fuzzy was strange.

"So what do you say? Want to help me find her?"

I wanted to say yes. I used to want him to ask me to go on vacation, or visit his work, or sleep at his house when I was younger, but I couldn't leave now.

"I can't," I said finally.

He nodded. His face still looked sad even though I think he was trying to hide it.

"She has school," Mom piped up, smiling too big. "She just joined the Game Development Club."

"Oh!" Dad's face lit up at that. "Game development? Is that like programming? That could be helpful for your college—"

I winced. I hated when he talked about college applications. He seemed to notice.

"I mean, that sounds fun."

Wes stayed for a bit longer, talking with Mom in the kitchen while I went back to practicing with my broom.

But it was hard to focus now that I was distracted by my dad's weird behavior and the news about Jo.

At 10:00 p.m., my alarm blared. It was time for the next phase.

I lay in bed, a soft night-light illuminating the watch. I imagined the giant sunflowers of Ten and wondered if they were somehow the Smoke Keepers of that clock world.

Will I really be a fox there? Jo thought so.

The watch hands spun and my eyelids grew heavy.

TEN

I awoke what felt like moments later to something bashing me in the head.

I sat up and realized that it was grass, a giant blade of grass that was about the same height as me and as wide as a door.

That is not what I expected when I practiced fighting with blades. I stood with a groan. It was hard to see past all the waving green stalks. Were they huge, or was I tiny?

I got my answer when I saw my feet, because they didn't look anything like my real feet. They were big and black and *furry*. I was still wearing my pajamas, but my body was covered in fur too, brown fur with a white stripe down the middle, and I could feel two pointy ears sticking out the top of my head.

Could I really be a fox?

No, because I was standing on my hind legs. I didn't think foxes could do that.

Maybe—I stared down at my big legs and knees—*I'm a kangaroo?*

I tried to hop, but it wasn't very impressive.

What am I? No, you know what? Who cares?

I needed to find the Smoke Keeper and I needed to do it now.

"Hello?" I called out, taking a few uneasy steps forward.

"Careful where you're walking, kid! You never know who's underfoot."

The high voice, reverberating from the depths of the grass, was small but piercing. I scuttled backward.

In this animal world it could be anything.

"Who are you?" I asked, trying to sound brave.

I could see a row of grass flattening in front of me. The blades fell forward, collapsing to the ground as if being run over by an oncoming tractor. I struggled to listen for footsteps as the thing approached me, but I heard nothing except for a dragging sound; whatever this creature was, it didn't have feet.

What slithered on the ground? An image of a big snake appeared in my mind. I wanted to run, but then the voice called out:

"The better question is, what are you doing in my house?"

The final row of grass fell forward, revealing the intruder: a snail whose head was as tall as my belly.

A giant talking snail wasn't the weirdest thing I had seen in the clock realms, but somehow—his beady black eyes stretched on the long antennae sprouting from his wet head—it felt strange anyway.

I backed away as the antennae bent toward me.

"Who are you?"

"I'm R-Rosemary," I stuttered, trying to compose myself as I took a queasy step toward him. I wanted to be brave. There was something particularly embarrassing about being a scaredy-cat (or whatever I was) in front of a snail.

"That's odd. You don't look like a rose, you look like a squirrel."

"A squirrel?" I leaned over to check my reflection in the gleam of his slimy shell.

Oh, man, I really am a squirrel.

"Rosemarys don't eat snails, do they?"

"No," I said quickly, trying to erase the memory of eating escargot at Wes and Cindy's wedding out of my head (just in case snails could read minds).

The snail stretched his head forward and squished

his mouth down on my furry arm. I gasped as a round sucker slurped at my skin before he lifted his head again, retreating.

"Ahh!" I wobbled backward, falling to the dirt. My heart was pounding like crazy.

"It seems snails don't eat Rosemarys either. What a shame." He wrapped his long neck around a blade of grass, nibbling off a bite before looking at me once more. "Palate cleanser" was all he said before sliding around in a circle.

"Anyway, Rosemary, stay out of my house." He slid over the ground all around me. "Everything the slime touches is mine."

"Fine, I'll leave you alone, but on one condition."

He stopped, his eyes wiggling.

"Where is your Smoke Keeper?"

His head shrunk back into his shell.

"Oh no, the only thing worse than big, furry intruders is the Smoke Keeper."

"Please," I begged, knowing I didn't have much time tonight, with Mom waking me up so early in the morning.

The snail began crawling away. *No, I can't lose him!*

I bounded after him. On my four legs I was much faster than he was. I hopped in front of him, stopping his retreat.

"If you don't show me, then maybe I *will* eat you."

I hadn't really meant it, and I felt guilty when his eyes popped wide, but I had to get to the Smoke Keeper.

"Fine. I'll take you to the Wall. That's where she lives. But I won't stay with you."

I followed him, careful to watch for any traps, until the grass finally ended. The field gave way into a clearing that felt very familiar.

I was sure I knew this place. It looked just like a painting Jo had made. I knew every inch of it, from the dirt on the ground, scattered with glittering white rocks, to the shadowy shapes looming overhead. I turned my face up to meet them—and immediately regretted it.

Staring down at me were the faces of humongous sunflowers, each as tall as a building, lined up in a row. And all of them were towering over me, the long stems craned straight down.

"What are those?" I gasped, pointing above us.

"Eep!" The snail slid back into the grass, hiding. "Those are the Wall. They suck up all the Smoke they can get and grow taller and taller."

"*Those* are the Wall?"

I looked closer and saw that the dark centers of the flowers were really swirling masses of multicolored smoke.

"Sure they are. But be vigilant. The Queen doesn't like it when critters get close to the Wall. She patrols it all day long, and she'll drop you right into one of the flowers if she catches you."

Then I noticed the big globs of smoke falling from the centers of the flowers, like pollen.

One burst in my face, making me feel Smoke Sick and woozy.

"Watch out, Rosemary! They'll suck you up!"

I backed away, far enough from the flowers that they couldn't reach me anymore, and shook off the dizziness.

"But where's the—"

As soon as I said it, the air was filled with buzzing.

"Run!" the snail warned me.

Floating down from the sky was a massive yellow bee—bigger than I was, with hollow eyes and black wings.

She's the Queen Bee, I realized all at once. And I also knew: she'd seen me.

I ran away from her, farther into the clearing, as fast as my four little legs would carry me. I was suddenly aware of my long, bushy tail as it slid across the ground, helping me balance as I bounded faster and faster.

The buzzing became louder, and the sky grew dark.

She was right above me.

I felt her legs grip my back, picking me up into the air. I yelped, unable to get away.

She was bringing me closer to the flowers. They stared at me in anticipation.

I craned my body to try to see her more clearly.

Where is her smoke? I just need to get a little bit.

This close to her, I could see wisps of pearly smoke in the fur that covered her round body.

I tried to reach for some, but it disappeared as soon as my back paw touched it. There wasn't enough of it.

She hovered over a flower, its petals stretched out wide and the swirling middle ready to devour me whole. I figured she planned to drop me straight into it.

I couldn't let that happen.

"*What* are you?" she buzzed.

"Your worst nightmare," I said, spinning and biting her leg, picturing Rambo.

The buzz became a hiss as she let go. I kicked off her body, arcing myself out of the way of the snapping flower bud, straight down its long stem.

I looked up to see the Queen skid along the flowers, sucking up their power, as she followed me. I also noticed her fur getting fluffier as it picked up pearly smoke pollen.

The more she picked up, the faster she flew.

That's it!

I stopped to pull the Smoke Ball from my pocket. Then I fitted the chain in my teeth and zoomed up a stem directly toward the Queen.

I heard her angry buzz, and I saw her outstretched legs and knifelike stinger, and they scared me, but they didn't stop me.

I jumped from flower to flower—just fast enough that the buds couldn't close on me. The Queen followed, collecting pollen along the way.

When it seemed like enough, I waited then jumped as high as I could.

This better work.

The Queen screamed as I landed on her back. I had to balance myself as she flew in zigzags, trying to throw me off.

I pulled the Smoke Ball from my teeth and clicked it open. A puff of smoke pollen on her fur sucked straight into it. The Smoke Ball now glistened with pearly energy too.

I did it.

"Grah!"

I lost my balance as the Queen bucked me backward. I couldn't stop myself as I careened toward the ground, falling in a heap in the dirt.

I could hear the Queen coming closer, but I was too tired to get up again.

I crawled, but I was too slow. The Queen was swooping in.

Seconds before her feet could latch on to me or her stinger could pierce me, I felt something else pick me up by the scruff of my neck and drag me forward, fast and low to the ground.

I screamed in surprise.

What is this thing?

The creature mumbled something, but its mouth was too full of my fur to make out what it said.

My head bobbed as it carried me. I could see the Queen flying behind us, zigzagging ever closer.

My captor dove into the tall grass, then suddenly stopped, breathing hard, still holding me underneath the cover of a bent blade.

I peeked out to see the Queen hovering above . . . then she flew away, searching for us.

The animal finally dropped me. I wanted to say thanks, but as soon as I'd gotten my footing, it was gone, running through the grass.

"Wait!" I whispered, following it. I caught a glimpse of orange fur.

Orange fur? Could it be?

"Stop!" I called, a bit louder now. "Jo? Is that y—"
I felt my whole body shake.
"No, not yet."
I could feel it—I was waking up.
"Jo!"
Then another shake and another.
I couldn't get away.

THE FIRST AND LAST MEETING OF THE GAME DEVELOPMENT CLUB

Someone was shaking my shoulder. I didn't want to open my eyes, desperate for a last glimpse of the creature that had saved me.

It has to be Jo, right? Why else would that thing have dragged me away from the Smoke Keeper like that?

"Come on, Rose, *you're* the one who wanted to wake up this stinking early!"

I felt the watch in my first, and I curled my fingers around it tightly. *At least I conquered another hour. When all of this weirdness is over, maybe I can go back to Ten and find that orange animal.*

My eyes blinked open.

"Oh, you're awake. Phew." Mom blew her bangs out of her face. "I'll give you fifteen minutes. We're already late."

I sat up quickly. "Late? What time is it?"

"Five fifteen. Hurry up!"

I stumbled into the church. My shirt was on backward, my sneakers were mismatched, and my backpack bulged like a turtle shell behind me.

I hadn't had time to waste getting ready—we only had until tomorrow to get to five more worlds.

I stopped, out of breath, in front of Alejandro, who was lying on a pew with his tablet.

"You're here!"

"I'm late."

He shrugged, setting his tablet aside with a smile. "We still have plenty of time."

I glanced at the tablet; it was already 5:40. *No, we don't.*

"So what do you want to do now? Draw a cover image? Come up with a title?" he asked.

I wanted to explain to him how desperate I was, how fast we had to work, but that would only make things harder. I breathed in deeply, preparing myself to continue lying.

"I want to brainstorm," I said.

"Oh. So, like, talk?"

"Actually, I need to dream up my . . . brainstorm."

"So you came here to"—he quirked his head to the side—"sleep?"

"Yeah?" I grimaced.

A moment later he burst into laughter before nodding. "Don't worry, I get it. I'm tired too."

It took us five minutes to set up a makeshift bed below one of the pews. I'd stuffed my backpack with a pillow and blanket. We'd worked it out. I was going to sleep underneath the pew. Then, when he heard me say his name, he'd knock on the wooden seat above me to wake me up.

I would tell him all the details he needed to know to keep developing the game, then I'd go back to sleep, and we'd do it all over again.

"You ready?" I asked, glancing at the time on his tablet again: 5:52.

"This is maybe the weirdest thing anyone has asked me to do, but . . ." He smiled. "I like weird. Let's go."

"Roger." I saluted him, sliding underneath the bench.

Tucked away in the dark, I felt the fear creep in. It was already getting so late, what if I couldn't fall asleep?

I felt the adrenaline rush through my body, making my skin jitter. So much had to happen today or else Jeremiah would be gone forever.

It's too much pressure! I'll never fall asleep.

I pulled out the watch. 5:54.

Six minutes.

Watching the hands did relax me, like it usually did, but it wasn't enough to overcome my fear. I followed the second hand spinning around and around, and I listened to the scratching of Alejandro's pencil above me, doing his homework.

5:58.

I clenched the watch to my chest, feeling its warmness spread through me, and I imagined the big stone head in the green, grassy field. I imagined it like I was really there.

Alejandro wasn't scratching on paper anymore; it was the sound of rocks scratching against one another.

My toes didn't flutter through the fringe of the blanket; instead, I felt soft, dry grass.

It wasn't wood I smelled or concrete.

It was fresh dirt and stones below.

FIVE

opened my eyes—but instead of seeing the underside of the pew, I was bathed in the shadow of something gigantic.

I stood up to see the massive thing *running directly toward me.*

I had to stop myself from screaming as I rolled out of the way. Seconds later a giant gray stone head, as big as a truck, stomped down in the spot I'd just vacated. Then it thrust back upward, followed by wisps of sandy-colored smoke.

I looked around to see a field of stone heads in rows, some white, some gray, like a giant chessboard surrounding me.

"Knock his block off! Knock his block off! Knock his

block off!" a jolly, deep voice shouted from above. It was a bald old man sitting atop one of the white stone heads. Little legs poked out below, just like they had in the picture from the book.

The running stone slammed down onto another giant rock just diagonal of me.

There was a loud crack. One of the white rocks split in half, its two pieces falling down to reveal the plain-looking woman inside. The stone was hollow now, and she bent to retrieve the pieces and carry them on her shoulders.

"Yay!" The old man leaped to his feet, causing the stone head holding him to stumble. "Guards, take her to the Wall!"

"No, please," the woman begged as two stone heads grabbed her from either side and dragged her through the grass and out of sight.

The crowd of stone faces was silent, but the old man cheered again and shouted, "Losers are weak, and weaklings get eaten by the Wall, isn't that right?"

None of the stone heads replied, but he giggled. "I love a good game of checkers!"

As he bent over, laughing, I caught a glimpse of a crown perched on his head.

He's the King. The Smoke Keeper.

I had to get to him fast—I needed to wake up before 6:00.

"Now it's my turn!" The man stomped on the stone head below him, which hulked into movement. It trudged toward a shivering gray head.

The old man snarled when it reached him, and he jumped so hard that clouds of tan smoke shot from his feet. He landed on the gray stone, splitting it straight in half, revealing a shaking boy underneath.

The white stone head bent down to catch the King, who scrambled back up it.

"I win! Guards!"

Two more guards took the crying boy away.

The King laughed again. "Who wants to try to beat me next?"

Feeling a momentary surge of bravery I didn't know I had, I leaped from my hiding spot.

"I do?"

"Who?" the Smoke Keeper cried, peering out into the field. "I can't see you."

I ran closer. As my feet pounded against the ground, they felt stronger than normal. I looked down—the harder I stepped, the more puffs of brown smoke leaked from my shoes.

"Where is her head?" the Smoke Keeper cried. "Cheating! Everyone besides the King must wear a head! It's not fair!" The Smoke Keeper pointed at me. "Seize her!"

Two more massive stones broke away from the game board and stomped toward me.

I had to do something. I didn't have time for guards. I needed to get up to the Smoke Keeper.

"Hit him with a sledgehammer," the imaginary Alejandro in my head whispered. But I didn't have a sledgehammer. Maybe here, however, my fists were close enough. I could feel the power running through them, and I got into Jackie Chan position, my knees bent, ready to fight.

"I got this," I whispered.

As soon as the first guard reached me, I kicked off the ground, using my new leg strength to fly into the air. A cloud of smoke shot behind me as I bounced off the guard's rock face.

"Why is her smoke that color? Grab the child! Grab her!" the King screamed.

I pinged back and forth between the guards' heads, leaping over their arms every time they tried to snatch me.

In my last jump I managed to kick off one guard's

arm and scramble to the top of his flat head. He looked from side to side, but I used all the strength in my fingers to hold on.

I could hear the gasps and whoops of the onlooking checkers pieces. I slowly straightened my legs, balancing on the head like it was a surfboard.

The King growled.

"Losers! You're all *weaklings*. Do I have to do *everything* myself?" He stomped again toward me. "To the girl!"

His stone head lurched forward while I leaped from head to head, away from him, until I got to the final row. I jumped off the last head onto the grass.

"King me!" I cried.

I hoped the King would follow me onto the ground from his perch. It seemed like my odds of fulfilling my mission would be much better down here than atop a giant head.

"All right, I will," the Smoke Keeper snarled. He leaped off his stone head straight to the ground, stalking toward me.

"You think you can win against me, *little girl*?"

As he approached, I knew I couldn't. I couldn't win against this tall man, with his hollow eyes and the puffs of smoke steaming off him. I barely even knew how to use my powers here.

"No, I don't," I said honestly.

"Then why," he snarled, his long teeth peeking out from a white beard, "are you challenging me?" He thrust an arm out, pinning my neck to the stone head behind me.

I used all of my strength to push against him, and he responded in kind, releasing his strength magic into a cloud around my throat.

"Because I don't have to beat you to win," I whispered, my windpipe crushed beneath his grip.

I managed to thrust the Smoke Ball into the cloud, absorbing his tan smoke.

"Wha—!" he shouted, letting go as he reached for the Smoke Ball. As soon as his hand released me, I let out the loudest, strongest shout I could: "Alejandro!"

Boom.

Smoke flooded me as I screamed again. "Alejandro!" The Smoke Keeper covered his ears.

Boom.

I heard a stone head shatter behind me.

Boom.

I startled awake, gasping for air. Alejandro was still knocking the pew above me, making the whole bench rattle.

"You okay down there, Rose? Any news from dream-land?"

"Yeah," I croaked, still groggy from sleep. "Big stone heads. White and gray. The King makes them play checkers. The losers are killed."

"But did you find out if the people are in the heads, bent over under the heads, or just *are* the heads?"

"In the heads."

"Perfect, that's all I needed to know. Thanks, Rose!"

"You got it." I stretched in my pillow fort, preparing for the next battle. "What time is it?"

"Uh, six eighteen."

I wasn't in there for too long. Good.

"I'm going back," I said, straightening my blanket back over me.

"Good luck," Alejandro said with a laugh.

If only you knew.

I clicked open the watch. *What was Six again?* I thought, my eyes already half closed. *Oh, yes, the apple. Fleck.*

I smiled thinking about her, and before I knew it, I was gone again.

SIX

W ell whatten we got here?"

The smell of dirt wafted over me in a wave. I looked up to see the farmer from the picture, only now he seemed different. His cheeks sucked in over sharp bones, his eyes were practically holes, and his teeth were long and rotten.

"You popped up out of nowhere!"

As soon as he said it, he started glowing with red smoke. Before I could whip the Smoke Ball out and get the heck out of there, he began to grow, as tall as a house.

"That must make you an outsider, huh? Ain't never seen one like you before. How did you get here?"

He snatched me up in one of his big, meaty hands and held me up so that I could see the rows of apple trees around us, tended to by hundreds of tiny people, picking giant apples. Surrounding the farm was the long, swirling Wall, like a fence.

We're so close to it, I have to get away.

"Time to meet the Wall, outsider."

I tried to remember Alejandro's advice: use a wheat stem to make him sneeze. But there was no wheat in sight, only apples, and we were getting closer and closer to the Wall.

But I had one idea.

I didn't know how to shrink, but I held my body in tight and imagined it. I imagined getting smaller, the way I tried to picture images before I drew them, the way Jo had taught me.

I tried to imagine it was real, what it felt like.

"What in *tarnation*?"

"Oops!" I had succeeded in growing small, but in doing so, I'd slipped right through the farmer's fingers.

As he fumbled for me, I climbed up one of his arms, heading straight for a place I didn't even want to think about: his dirty, crooked nose.

"Where are you—"

"Ha!" I lunged at his face and grabbed one long nose hair.

"Let go of me, rat!" He shook his head from side to side before stopping to take in a big breath.

"Ahhh . . ." *This is it!* ". . . CHOO," he sneezed.

At the same time, I imagined being bigger now—just big enough to pinch his nose as he blew, causing his ears to burst with red smoke.

I flung the Smoke Ball sideways to catch the smoke, then immediately tucked it away and jumped off him.

I hit the ground and ran into the orchard.

"Why, you little . . . !"

I grew to my regular size as I ran . . .

Boom.

. . . hiding from his giant, stomping feet . . .

Boom.

. . . screaming the whole way. "Alejandro!"

Boom.

"I'm awake!" I cried, bathed in sweat. "I was running from the farmer. You were right. I had to make him sneeze."

"Oh?"

"But there was no wheat. I had to make myself tiny, then swing from his nose hair."

"Gross."

"I know. What time is it now?"

"Four minutes past seven."

"Perfect. Good night."

"Good night," Alejandro repeated, chuckling again.

It had become a rhythm. I didn't even have to prepare myself as I descended into the vision of the metal-covered woman.

SEVEN

Mine! Mine! *Mine!*" A horrible shriek made my eyes shoot open, and it was good they did, because I was falling down a steep slide.

"Whoa!" I managed to catch the edge of the slide, barely holding on with my fingertips. When I looked down, I saw the swirling energy of the Wall below.

Below? How can it be below?

"Give that to me!" a voice hissed from above. I looked up to see a massive maze of metal tracks running in many directions. A woman, glittering with metal stuck to every part of her body (there were chains, rings, cutlery, and even a teakettle), stalked above me. She hummed with silver energy—especially her feet every time she stepped.

Maybe, I considered, *she magnetized herself to the track?*

I tested it myself, trying to magnetize my feet to the metal slide. It worked. I stood up (or sideways, I guess) and followed the woman.

She was trudging toward a girl who was running from her. On the little girl's back was a frying pan.

"Mine!" The woman held out a hand. The pan shot to her arm, sticking to the mass of metal around her. "It's all mine!"

"I'm sorry, Your Highness, you can have anything you want," the girl squeaked. But she was too late. The woman snatched the girl by the arm, yanking her free of the metal rail. The girl screamed.

I positioned myself on a track below them. When I looked up, I could see their feet, glowing silver above me.

I squinted higher and caught a glimpse of the woman's long-toothed smile.

I tentatively stuck my feet to the wall of the track and climbed up it, crouched, quiet, taking big magnetized steps.

I held my Smoke Ball to her feet, sucking up the silver energy.

Yes, that's it.

I was about to scream, to signal Alejandro, when the girl above me did instead.

I watched as the Queen let go of her. The girl fell straight toward the Wall below us.

As she passed me, I reached out. I didn't want to see someone else get sucked into the Wall.

I didn't catch her, but a wave of brown smoke bloomed from my hand, enveloping hers and shooting it to the metal—magnetized stuck.

She looked at me, out of breath, as shocked as I was.

"Who are you?" the Queen shouted above me.

"Run," I said to the girl. She did, detaching her body from the metal and dropping to a rail below.

The Queen's face dangled through the track above mine.

"Now your turn." Her clawed hand reached for me, plucking my hanging fingers off, one by one.

Boom.

Wait, I thought, already feeling dizzy.

Boom.

I hadn't even said Alejandro's name yet.

Boom.

"Rose! Hey, Rose! Come on!" Alejandro was rapping on the wood above me. I rubbed the dream away. "We're going to be late for class."

Good thing I managed to get the smoke in time.

We left the church quickly. I didn't have time to pack up my pillow and blanket, but it didn't matter. I couldn't keep the big smile from stretching across my face. I had done it—three worlds in as many hours. I felt brave, and strong, and important. Now there were only two worlds left. With the pictures from the book, Jo's instructions, and Alejandro's help, I felt unstoppable.

I was going to save Jeremiah after all.

As Alejandro and I rushed to class, I told him all about my quick and dirty adventures, and he showed me the outline of the game he was making, based on my dreams.

"It's cool—it'll be like *Warp Jump* and *Torch Throwers* and your new elements all mixed together."

It actually looked pretty fun.

By the time we entered the building, the first bell had just rung and we had to push past masses of kids rushing to class. We were so busy talking that I didn't care that other people were bumping into me.

"No, you're not just extra strong with your hands, see? It's like everything. You can run faster because your legs are stronger, and you can scream louder because your throat is stronger, and—" I was saying.

"Wait, I don't think that's how you scream," Alejandro interrupted.

"Well, whatever, you get it—it's just all of you. All of you gets stronger."

"Yeah, that's cool! We can add in double jumps for that level so you can go extra high, and maybe there can be a—*whoa!*"

Alejandro stumbled into me. I caught his shoulder as the culprit breezed past us. Samantha had bumped into him, flouncing after a bobbing blond ponytail that hurried in front of her. *Fallon.*

"But I don't understand," Samantha whined to Fallon's back. "Why are *you* here?"

I listened as we followed them to class, curious.

"I told you, I was bored at home."

"Bored? You were *bored*?"

Fallon didn't answer. I could hear the eye roll in Samantha's words. "Shouldn't you be with Jeremiah, though?"

Fallon turned to look at her, to say something. I could see her face scrunch up in pain, but then she turned around again. "I just wanted to come back to school."

I wanted to say something, but I worried I would make it worse. *Maybe I'm not unstoppable after all.*

"I'm just saying, if it were *my* brother, I'd be with him."

Fallon stayed quiet after that, but Alejandro spoke

beside me. "It's easy to say that you'd do something when you don't know what it actually feels like."

Samantha stopped, forcing us to stop too, as she spun around. Her face looked like she'd sucked on a lemon.

"This has nothing to do with you."

Alejandro shrugged, mimicking her words. "I'm just saying." Then he continued, "I've had lots of bad things happen—stuff that I never would have understood before I knew what they felt like."

"Oh, okay, so your brother is in the hospital too?" Samantha spat at him.

"Of course not," he answered.

I stayed by Alejandro's side, feeling more confident than usual with him next to me. Brave enough to tell Samantha, "But that doesn't mean she's a bad sister for coming to school. I know that Fallon's a really good sister, actually."

Fallon caught my eye.

"Whatever, I don't have to listen to you," Samantha sneered, looking at me. "You don't even have any friends."

"I'm her friend," Alejandro said.

For a moment I thought I saw Fallon grimace, but I was distracted when Samantha turned back to Alejandro and snickered, "Oh yeah, *you*. I remember you."

"Huh?" I turned to Alejandro, expecting to see him

as confused as I was, but instead, his face went pale.

"What do you mean?" Fallon asked.

"You don't remember him? Alejandro Fuentes. He went to kindergarten with us."

He did? I don't remember that. I looked at him again. *He never said anything about it.*

"Then he had to leave because he burned his house down. My mom told me all about it. The news said that his dad got, like, really hurt from it."

"No, he didn't," I automatically snapped.

"Ask him," Samantha snapped back, spinning around. "I don't have to listen to any of you."

Samantha stormed off into the classroom just as the final bell rang.

"Thanks, you guys" came Fallon's small voice before she rushed into class after her.

I stayed where I was with Alejandro. We were late, but I didn't care. I was reeling from everything that had just happened.

"Is that true?" I asked him. He stood across from me, his head down.

"Remember . . . ," he said after a pause. "Remember when I told you that I was born here? But that there was an accident and we had to move?"

I nodded, not sure what to say.

"I really didn't mean to do it. Then we had to leave so that we could live with our family. So they could take care of my dad. He got burned really bad." He looked up at me. "It was an accident. A big accident. There have been lots of accidents. I'm just . . ." He sighed. "I'm just really unlucky."

"That's okay. I understand," I said.

He raised his head.

"I've been really unlucky too," I told him. "And I've made some bad mistakes myself." I couldn't stop the image of Jeremiah's lifeless face from floating into my mind.

"Really? You're not scared off by me?" he asked quietly.

"You've been nice to me, Alejandro. Nicer than anyone else. An accident doesn't change that."

He smiled. Before he could say anything else, however, Mr. Topinka's bald head popped out the cracked door.

"What are you two doing outside? You're late!"

THE LOST HOUR

The rest of school was the best day I've had in a long time. Alejandro was my first real friend in forever, and after the fight in the hall we felt even more comfortable with each other, I think. We talked about our "game" all day, and I used our ideas to prepare for the final two hours: the mysterious Twelve and, lastly, back to Eleven.

I convinced Mom to let me stream a movie about knights, swords, and fighting that night. I wondered if the castle in Twelve would be like the one in the movie.

I would probably have to fight there—a duel, maybe?

That felt extra scary because I didn't even know what my powers were going to be there. I had no way to plan for that world.

And yet, I had so quickly conquered the other worlds . . . was there any way I could do it again?

I stayed up until midnight. I was beyond tired when I crawled into bed, but my nerves kept me up until Mom quietly checked on me at 12:30 on her own way to bed.

I watched the minute hand on the watch.

I imagined the castle from the missing petal.

I wondered how I was going to find the Smoke Keeper. It was easy with the other hours because that Amisi guy had put the Kings and Queens in the book so I could picture them as I fell asleep.

Probably, though, the King or Queen of Twelve would be in the castle, right? Yeah. That must be why Jo didn't leave me a hint. It would probably be obvious.

I yawned, rolling onto my side.

I was about to go there, to see the castle—a real castle.

I closed my eyes and held the watch to my chest. That was all it took as the warmth of the watch pulsed in time with the beat of my heart.

TWELVE

'd imagined a fairy-tale sky, with cotton-ball clouds and singing birds. Not this.

I squinted, standing up. Everything was dark. There was nothing here. It was a wasteland. A desert. The sky was filled with thick clouds of sickly yellow dust. It was hard to see anything but outlines in it.

"Hello?" I called out. But my voice barely carried through the dusty air.

As I started to explore, I stumbled over a slab of bricks, worn from age.

I crouched to get a better look. They were yellow, like the dust in the air, and as my finger ran along the surface of one, the top of the brick dissolved into more dust, falling to the sand below.

This was a crumbling place. A forgotten place.

"Hello!" I shouted again.

This can't be right, I thought as I walked farther into the nothingness, blinking back against the dust.

I held the watch, now a glowing Smoke Ball, in front of me in an attempt to light my way. *This isn't Twelve.* It couldn't be, where was the castle? The trees? The people?

A horrible realization turned in my belly. *I must have fallen asleep at the wrong time.* But I'd been to so many other worlds, and none of them looked like this.

There were slick stones under my feet. I bent down low to brush away the sand and saw that I was standing on a pocked-tile walkway. At the end of it sat a very tall, wide building. The roof and walls had caved in, as though having lost in a vicious battle.

But there was no mistaking the drawbridge in front of it or the towering stained-glass windows that remained on one side and were scattered across the ground on the others in shards.

This was the castle. Or, at least, it used to be.

No. This was a trick. It had to be.

I walked over the drawbridge toward the entrance. I could see the structures more clearly now, holding up my Smoke Ball to light the places where solid walls and towers should have been.

Then I went through the front door, bracing myself. At least the Smoke Keeper had to still be alive, right? They lived forever. But the inside of the castle looked no different from the outside.

"Mr. King? Mrs. Queen?" I called out. "Anyone?" I waited, but no answer came.

Maybe . . . maybe if I could figure out what the magic was here, I could use it to find someone?

I tried drawing on the ground, punching a wall, holding a brick and willing it to grow or shrink. I tried to fly, to scream, to do *anything*. Nothing worked. I was just a normal person here, and I hated it. I didn't know what to do.

I wanted to give up.

Jo used to say that, in Three, if you felt sad or angry, a fire would light beneath your feet, sucking you into it. If you didn't get out fast enough, you'd burn up. The only way out was if you managed to make yourself get rid of the anger—which is a particularly hard thing to do when, you know, you're being *murdered by your own feelings*.

She used to remind me of that whenever I complained about something: if you let one bad thing get to you, then you're bound to attract all kinds of other bad things.

I sighed. Saving Jeremiah would be absolutely impossible if I couldn't find the Smoke Keeper of Twelve, so that's what I had to do.

Get out of the fire. I was going to make things right.

I took a step forward and promptly slipped on something. I screamed as I fell hard on my tailbone.

"Ow!" My back hurt from the fall, my head hurt from the stress, and my lungs hurt from the dust in the air.

Never mind, you know what? Let the fire eat me. I'm basically the unluckiest girl in the world.

Just as soon as I thought that, though, my skin felt funny. Warm. I looked down to see that my whole body glistened with smoke.

My magic. It's working.

I sat up and saw that something else also gleamed with brown smoke: the thing I had slipped on.

I scrambled over to see. It was a portrait, I think, a big one. I could just see the head of someone underneath the thick layer of sand and debris.

I rubbed my sleeve over it, revealing the face.

I gasped.

I knew that face—that mustache and those eyes. It was Amisi, and he was wearing a crown.

I picked up the painting with shaky hands.

But how? And where is he?

"Amisi!" I called out, desperate.

I searched the castle all night, the grounds, holding his picture and screaming his name the whole time: "Amisi!"

But still, I found no one.

THE LAST-DITCH EFFORT

By the time I woke up, I was certain of one thing: Jeremiah was going to die.

I hadn't found Amisi, or anyone else for that matter. There was no way for me to collect the smoke.

I'd failed.

I lay back in bed. There was no point getting up. Even if I went back into Twelve at noon and miraculously found the Smoke Keeper that time, I would have missed my chance at getting into Eleven this morning. And if I saved Eleven until tonight, it would be too late—there was no way I could guarantee saving Jeremiah before the deadline. I needed the smoke from Twelve first.

It's already the last day.

I stayed in bed until Mom knocked on my door to get me up for school, too sad to move.

. . .

I trudged to class wearing my pajama pants. I hadn't had the energy to change. Kids stared at me, but I didn't care.

What's the point anymore? It's over. Even if I came up with an excuse to get out of class before 11:00, it didn't matter without the smoke from Twelve.

I collapsed in my seat before the bell even rang—a first for me—then laid my head down, but moments later someone was tapping on it.

"What?" I asked, annoyed, expecting Samantha to make fun of my clothes or Mr. Topinka to tell me to wake up.

Instead, it was Alejandro. His eyes were big and his voice was frantic.

"Where did you get the idea for this?"

He pulled a painting out of his bag—one of my paintings that I'd been working on in the church. It was of Eleven's Smoke Keeper.

"Oh, it's just a character from a story that my aunt used to tell me. Why do you have it?"

"Don't get mad," he said, gesturing wildly as he spoke, "but I was going through your paintings this morning to try to find one for the cover art of our game, and I saw this one . . . and I swear"—he handed me the painting before leaning in close to whisper—"I know this story too. That's called a Smoke Keeper, right?"

I bolted upright. "How do you know that?" I'd never used that term with him before; during our brainstorming sessions I'd always referred to the characters like the farmer and the metal lady as just the "king" or "queen" of that level.

"Look." His hand was shaking from either nervousness or excitement as he pulled something else out of his bag. "After I saw your painting, I went home and then came back with this."

He handed me a small stack of thick paper, tinged with age. A drawing of something unmistakable was on the first page.

Long, cracked teeth, sheared nose, empty eyes, and a crown. Underneath in a looping cursive it read *Smoke Keeper.*

"How did you get this?" I asked, flipping to the next page.

"It's been passed down in my family for generations. It belonged to my dad—his grandmother gave it to him. She said her father made it."

I continued flipping through the stack. I knew this paper. I knew what this was.

"I thought he came up with this story himself, but is

it like a legend or something? I've never heard anything like it apart from these drawings and notes. Where did you hear about it?"

Though it was considerably more worn and the drawings were sketchier—made by a less talented hand—there was no denying it: this was the missing part of Jo's book.

"And what was the name of your great-grandmother's father?" I asked, ignoring his question.

"Oh, him? Uh. Olaf, I think. Olaf Amisi."

My heart thudded in my chest. This wasn't possible. *How could this be?*

There were sketches that I had never seen before, including one with a sparkling kingdom—a place where the clouds looked perfectly puffy and the trees dripped with leaves of silk. Like the kind of place that didn't exist anymore. Like it was magic.

There were notes scribbled all along the sides: *Harold, everything is white like marble. The air smells like cut grass. The people are golden. They have the ability to control luck. But if you use too much one way, it has to make itself equal again.*

Above the largest and most detailed drawing of the realm looped the words *Twelve: My Kingdom.*

These must have been the notes that Amisi had

given to Harold Marks, my own ancestor, when he illustrated the book.

This was all too much to process. I needed to think. What were the chances? Could I really be that lucky?

The bell rang, but I didn't have time for class.

Clutching the pages close to my chest with one arm, I grabbed Alejandro's wrist with the other and pulled him toward the door. On the way out I bumped into Fallon.

"Oh, hey, sorry—gotta go," I mumbled, brushing past her.

"Where?" she called after me.

But I was too frantic to answer. I needed to get him to the church—somewhere private we could chat.

Once we got inside, I started splaying the pages across a long pew. These pictures were not in Jo's book, but I was certain what they were. There was a Wall made of energy, a sword with twelve stones embedded in the hilt, and a diagram showing how to melt the sword down into a watch. Is this how the watch was first made? It must have been. Amisi used the sword to create it.

Alejandro wheezed behind me, catching his breath. "We're missing class, Rose. Why? Are we here just to talk about my father's book? Because it could have waited till lunch . . ."

"No, we don't have time. It can't wait till lunch." I spun around to look him straight in the eye. "Tell me everything you know about this book."

"Oh, uh, right. Okay. Well, like I told you, it belonged to my great-great-grandfather. He said he wrote the book for his daughter about his 'real home.'" Alejandro used finger quotes around that last part. "He claimed he was from this magical place and ended up in Arizona by accident. That's what my family says, anyway, and that he was planning to go back. So he was writing a book for his daughter so she'd remember him when he was gone."

"Why did he want to go back?"

"He told my great-grandma that there was a war going on there that he had to stop. He'd been fighting in it before some big blast of magic energy or something shot him here, into our world. I always thought that part was cool; it reminds me of this game actually—"

"And then what happened?" I cut him off, leaning forward.

"He just disappeared at some point, leaving behind these pages, his story, for his wife and daughter . . ."

I gasped. *Could he still be in Twelve?*

" . . . and a watch."

"What?"

"Oh, didn't you see that page?" He shuffled through the drawings spread out on the bench and picked one up. "Here." He handed me a page that included a diagram of a watch. I examined it closely.

"It wasn't just a picture—supposedly, there really was a watch and it looked just like that."

A round watch with twelve petals. The very same one my hand grazed over in my pajama pocket.

"What happened to it?" I asked.

"It was stolen."

"What? By who?"

Alejandro leaned over, leafing through the pages again. "Ah, here it is." On the back of a portrait of Amisi was taped a story from an old newspaper. No photos, just lettering that looked grainy and stamped on, with the headline MAN MISSING.

"After Amisi disappeared, no one ever found him. Rumors were that he'd been kidnapped. Days after he went missing, his wife said the watch was stolen from her room."

"Who did it?" My heart thumped so loud, I thought Alejandro must have been able to hear it.

Alejandro shrugged, lining the pages back up again.

"My dad's grandmother said it was a friend of his—some guy he'd hired to draw the pictures for his book."

I felt like I was sinking. I couldn't believe it.

"The friend got greedy or something. Amisi's wife thought the friend even killed him, so that he could steal the watch and the book. But it was never published—that's the weird thing." Alejandro got a confused look on his face, like something was dawning on him. "So how could you know about it too—the story?" he asked, staring at me.

My eyes slowly met his as I absorbed what he was saying.

The artist killed him. Stole his work and the watch.

"I think . . . I think it was *my* great-great-grandfather who was the illustrator."

"What?" Alejandro's eyebrows shot up. "Why would you think that?"

I dug my hand deep into my pocket and pulled out the watch, handing it to him with shaky fingers. I almost couldn't let it go. "Because this has been passed down in my family too."

Alejandro held the watch up to his wide eyes. Thoughts whirled around in my head. If Amisi was dead, there was no way I could get his smoke . . . unless . . . unless Alejandro really was his descendant. Then he would have the same royal blood, right? He'd be the King of Twelve now, even if he'd never been there. *Could this work?*

"Look," I said to Alejandro, "I know this is a lot to take in and it's going to sound totally nuts, but I think I need your help."

"With what?" His voice sounded shaky.

"The war your great-great-grandfather wanted to end."

He just stared at me. "What are you talking about?"

"I know it's hard to believe, but . . ." I groaned— this was not only utterly ridiculous, but impossible to explain. "I just need you to trust me. All those levels I was coming up with for our game, all those worlds? That was me using the watch to enter your grandpa's world."

"I don't believe it. That's *impossible.*"

I peered into his eyes. "I thought so too, but look." I gently took the watch back, clicking it open for him to see. "It's real. The watch from your family's story is *real.*"

Alejandro gasped, staring at the pictures under the petals. I was too scared to say anything more yet, worried he might not want to help me.

"And how do you plan to end this . . . war, exactly?" he finally asked.

"I told you that I'd made mistakes too, right?

Remember?" He nodded. I took a deep breath. "Well, I was the one who hurt Jeremiah." I reached down, picking up the sketch of Twelve's Wall. "He's stuck in there, and if I don't find a way to get him out of it by tonight, then he'll never wake up again."

After a long pause Alejandro looked up from the watch to me. "What do you need from me?"

"I need you to take a nap at eleven o'clock today. We'll have less than an hour, and we'll need all the time we can get."

At that his expression cracked. "A nap? But we're at school. How are we going to manage—"

Now that I knew he'd help, I didn't let him finish. "I have an idea . . . just trust me, okay?" My mind raced with possibilities. We'd sneak back into the building between first and second periods, then maybe we could do the impossible.

At 10:45, in Mrs. Lee's class, I started acting sick—taking shallow breaths, holding my face, swallowing real hard over and over. I was so nervous, I didn't have to fake the sweating or the shaking. With the watch safely in my pocket, I made my way to Mrs. Lee's desk and asked her if I could go to the nurse's office. One look at me and she reached into her desk for the hall pass. "Can Alejandro come with me?

I'm afraid I'm going to throw up on the way there."

She quickly signaled to Alejandro to follow me, no doubt eager to get the nauseated kid out of her classroom.

When we got to the nurse's office, it was empty. I couldn't believe it—it seemed like my luck really had changed. I collapsed on one of the flat beds in the back room and told Alejandro to take the one right next to it.

"Here. You hold on to the watch while I hold the end of the chain."

"What if I can't fall asleep?" he asked.

"You have to. As long as you fall asleep before noon, I'll find you. You remember what to think about before you fall asleep, though, right?" I'd coached him on our way back from the church that morning.

"Yes. A big graveyard in a swamp, like the one in your picture."

"Don't forget. If you don't imagine it right, you might not end up in the right place."

"I'll remember."

We lay on our sides, facing each other in our separate beds, the watch chain taut between us.

"But I'm not sleepy," he groaned.

"Trust me, if you open the watch and stare at it, it'll knock you right out."

"Really?"

"Yup, but wait until I fall asleep first, so I can help you once we get there."

"Okay," he said quietly.

I closed my eyes. I was more worried about my ability to fall asleep *without* the watch.

"Rose?"

"Yeah?"

"How amazing will it be if you're telling the truth?"

I opened my eyes, smiling back at him.

"Very amazing."

When I closed my eyes again, however, the smile slipped off. This was my last shot. I needed it to work.

I imagined the graveyard. I willed my thoughts and nerves to calm down, and I tried to pretend that I was lying on Jo's couch with her, watching the fire, feeling her fingers comb through my hair, and listening to her soft whisper.

"You see, Rose, there's a place where anything is possible, and when you go there, you will become more powerful than anyone you've ever met."

ELEVEN

I t was hot. That was the first thing I noticed—pure, slick heat running through my body.

I opened my eyes and was met by a dark sky washed with rainbows above. Below me was hard stone on top of warm, mossy ground. *No, not moss. Grogs. "Watch out for the Grogs,"* tickled Jonquil's voice at the back of my memory.

I sat up. Straight ahead were thick, marble cubes of white. The catacombs.

I made it.

I was too anxious to wait for Alejandro. I needed to make sure that Fleck, Jonquil, and Scape had all made it back safe from our fight with the Smoke Keeper.

I'll come back for him. He'll wait for me.

So I stumbled up the steps of the catacombs, winding through the maze, trying to remember how to get to the top.

"Fleck? Jonquil? Scape?" I kept calling their names as I drew deeper into the tunnels. But no one responded.

What if they've already been thrown into the Wall? Then I felt a hand wrap firmly around my upper arm and pull me straight into a cavern.

"Ahh!" I was pinned hard against the wall of the cave, my back to it, something thin pointed at my throat.

"Rose?"

The hand released me. When my eyes adjusted to the dark, I could make out a face.

Fleck.

I grabbed her in a hug, suddenly filled with relief. "Fleck! You're here! You're alive." It had only been a couple of days, but it had felt like I'd lost them all forever.

"Ugh, of course I am," she scoffed. She pulled away, and I saw that what was in her hand was Amisi's sword. She sheathed it in her belt, under her tunic. "You came back."

When I looked at her face again, it seemed tired, although I could see the hints of surprise in the way her eyebrows raised and her lips quirked up.

"Where are Jonquil and Scape?"

At the sound of my voice I heard small footsteps approach from the darkness, and the dirt-strewn face of Scape appeared.

Neither they nor Fleck quite met my eyes.

"And Jonquil?"

"He, uh . . . ," Fleck began, before sniffing. She seemed like she was trying to control herself enough to speak, but she finally gave up, looking to Scape.

"He got sick, Rose, trying to get your friend out. They caught him, and now he's in the Wall too."

Oh no, it's my fault.

"We'll get him back."

Fleck and Scape both looked at me, surprised.

"We can't," Fleck spat. Then I saw her eyes dart to the bulge of the Smoke Ball in my pocket. "Unless you got them?" Her eyes looked as though they had been lit from within—even her freckles seemed to sparkle.

"Well . . ." I pulled the Smoke Ball out. It glowed with all kinds of smoke.

Fleck leaned in to count the colors. "Ten? Only ten? We need all twelve!"

"I still need the smoke from Eleven; we can get that now."

"And how are you going to fly to Twelve?"

"I don't need to."

"Why not?" she challenged.

"Because the Smoke Keeper from Twelve died in the last war."

Fleck's and Scape's faces both fell. They looked small, crumpled, and ashen against the dark walls.

"So then we can't save them?"

"No, that's not it—I think I might have found someone."

"Who?"

"The new King of Twelve."

"But we need the smoke *now* to save your friend!" Fleck demanded.

"I know." I nodded. "The new King is coming."

"Coming? Coming where? Here?!"

"Yes, but . . ." Something flickered in the corner of my eye. I looked down. The Smoke Ball had disappeared.

Just like it did with Jeremiah. That must mean . . .

"He's here. Come on."

Fleck had directed us out of the maze with barking orders. She knew the catacombs better than anyone, I realized, as she pulled and pushed us through secret tunnels and shortcuts.

The three of us stood outside, feet sinking into the hot mud, heads whipping around. I didn't see Alejandro and worried that he'd ended up in the wrong place after all.

Please be here, please be here . . .

"Rose?"

We all turned to find Alejandro standing behind me. His mouth hung open and his eyes were wide. In his hand was the Smoke Ball.

"You made it!" I rushed to him.

"This place is . . ." His voice was quiet.

"Scary?" I asked.

"So. Cool." He breathed heavily, whipping around. "It's like we're *inside* a game. Did you see those tiny frogs?"

"We don't have time for this, Rosemary," Fleck scolded, approaching us. "Is this the one from Twelve or not?"

I turned to Alejandro, slightly worried about the answer. "We'll see. Alejandro, hold your nose and blow out your ears."

"What? Like this?" He held his nose and blew. A cloud of gold smoke shot into the air, covering the ground in sparkles.

When Alejandro opened his eyes, he gasped, "What was that?"

"That"—I grabbed the Smoke Ball from him, glad we'd both been holding it in the real world, and sucked in the gold energy—"is your smoke."

"My what?"

My thoughts drifted back to Amisi's book.

"You have the ability to control luck. But if you use too much one way, it has to make itself equal again."

"Luck?"

I nodded.

"That's weird, because I'd say that my whole life, I've been just about the unluckiest person alive."

He stared at the gold dots swirling around the Smoke Ball.

"So he really is the King," Fleck breathed out behind me.

"Wait, I'm a *king*—"

"There's no time," I cut him off, starting to sprint toward the forest, headed to the city. "We have to get smoke from Eleven's Smoke Keeper before we wake up!"

"Hey!" Fleck said, catching up to me and snatching my arm. "That's not the most efficient way to search for him, is it?"

"Why did you make it a dragon?" I asked.

"More fun than a bird, isn't it?" Fleck answered.

"Whoa!" Alejandro screamed behind me.

We soared over the city of Eleven, the party raging below us, on the back of a bronze dragon.

"What are we going to do when we find the Smoke Keeper?" I called out to Fleck ahead of me.

"Lure him to the beach, away from all the people."

"There he is!" Scape shouted. They were staring through a pair of binoculars they'd drawn out of wood.

Fleck pulled the reins in the dragon's mouth, sending us straight toward the ground. I closed my eyes. Alejandro screamed again behind me, and Scape whooped ahead.

My eyes flashed open, however, feet from the ground. We soared right over the heads of dancers who screeched in fear and approval, toward the Smoke Keeper, who lunged for my feet, hanging over the dragon's belly.

"There they are! Seize them!" the Smoke Keeper shouted.

We swooped back up into the air. I looked behind us—the Smoke Keeper followed.

I breathed in deeply. This was it. I had to get the Smoke Keeper's magic. *But how?*

I didn't have much time to think as we descended onto the beach below.

I just need to get him to draw something.

"Fleck," I shouted, "quick, draw a ship and sail out on the Mire. I'll find you."

"I will. But first"—she unbuckled the sheath from around her waist, fitting it around mine instead so that Amisi's sword now lay against my leg—"take this. If you get the chance, just destroy the Wall. Don't worry about us."

I nodded, trying to hold back my nerves. "Got it."

Alejandro fell to the ground as the dragon burst into purple smoke. He stood, dusting himself off, unnerved, before stepping to me.

"Rose, what's going on?"

"Go hide behind them." I pointed to the sleeping Islets on the sand. "And just stay safe. I'll wake you up when this is all over."

"It's the Smoke Keeper! He's coming!" Fleck shouted.

"Wait, where are you going?" Alejandro grabbed the sleeve of my sweatshirt.

"I have to do something. Now hurry—go hide."

I pushed him toward the Islets and watched until he crouched behind one, then turned back around to see the Smoke Keeper, alone, striding toward me on the sand.

"There you are. I've been looking for you."

I had to calm my breathing as I stood there, gathering strength from the blade poised on my hip. *I was meant to do this. I* can *do this.*

"You're too late," I shouted at him. "You've lost the rest of them already." I pointed to Fleck's white marble ship bobbing on the Mire.

"Oh, I'll get to them, but first"—he took three big steps to me, fast and frightening, but I held my ground—"I will take you to the Wall." He yanked me forward by my wrist, whispering in my ear, "Just like your little friends."

I stopped myself from shivering, facing him head-on. "And how do you plan to do that? Last time I destroyed your boat."

He smiled his long-toothed grin. "You think you're the only one who can do magic tricks?" He pulled me with him as he strode to the Islets.

As we approached the sleeping beasts, I saw Alejandro's eyes peeking out.

Oh no. Alejandro.

"Let go of me!" I shouted, trying to wrench my arm free. I just needed to distract him.

"Quiet!" the Smoke Keeper bellowed, whipping around and slicing my cheek with one of his long nails.

I yelped. I could feel a drop of blood streaming down.

"You cannot get away. I am indestructible, invincible." He leaned in close to my ear once more. "Give up."

I glanced over the Smoke Keeper's shoulder to see Alejandro hidden again. That's all I needed.

The Smoke Keeper stopped at an Islet, pulling a blade from his belt. He snarled at me, a smirk slitting across his thin, cracked lips. "Now it's time to make a ship you cannot meddle with."

"Stop!" I cried as he thrust the blade down on the Islet's shell.

But the Smoke Keeper kept carving as the Islet screamed. Blue smoke gathered in a cloud around his hand.

I tried to block out the sounds of pain as I dug the Smoke Ball out of my pocket with my free hand and held it up just long enough for the smoke to be absorbed.

Got it.

I stashed the Smoke Ball just in time, because moments later a blue ghostly shape shot out, onto the Mire's edge. Then it formed into a black ship.

"Come, child."

Now I just have to get free and put the Smoke Ball in the sword hilt.

With a hard yank of my hand at the same time as I stomped on the Smoke Keeper's foot, I broke free of his grip, whirling around like Indiana Jones.

Then I took off running just as the Islet shell behind

us blew up in a cloud of smoke. I used it as cover, darting for the other Islets.

The Smoke Keeper roared, tearing after me.

I pulled out the sword, then fumbled for the Smoke Ball in my pocket. But my hands were too slick with sweat, and the heavy sword fell.

Oh no!

"You!"

The Smoke Keeper descended upon me again, grabbing me by my neck this time and raising me into the air. I pulled against his hands with all my might, gasping for breath.

"I don't even care if the Wall gets you. I'll have enough smoke from your friends. You I will kill right here."

Still gasping for breath, my eyes rolled away, looking for something, anything, to help me. That's when I saw Alejandro. He was kneeling against the Islet, his hands clasped as if in prayer. I could just make out the word he was whispering.

"Please, please, please."

The Smoke Keeper's hand tightened around my neck, and I felt the world around me growing blurry.

No, I can't lose here.

My eyes were closing.

Then Alejandro started to glow gold.

Gold smoke shot from his head and surrounded the Islets sleeping next to him, waking them. They rose and turned toward us.

They screamed and ran.

It was another stampede.

How lucky.

"What the—" The Smoke Keeper was slammed, broadsided by one of the massive beasts. He dropped me as he went flying.

Gulping in air, I stumbled to my feet.

Alejandro ran to me. "I did it! I used my luck magic! Did you see?"

"Get. The. Sword," I wheezed, trying to regain my senses.

He hurried back and hefted it out of the sand. As soon as he held it, the sword, too, was surrounded by gold. He handed it to me. "Rose, here—"

But a long-fingered hand snatched it first.

"I see." The Smoke Keeper's arm reached between us. His legs were snapped from the impact, bowed inhumanly.

How did he get here so fast?

Snap. Snap.

With a thrust of his knees, his legs righted themselves, glowing with blue smoke.

"I told you," he hissed, "I am invincible."

Then he looked down at the glowing sword. "You thought you could defeat me with this?" He smirked, heaving the sword into the Mire.

"No!" I screamed, running toward it. But I was too late.

The gold melted upon impact, then sank into the dark depths below.

I stared after it, completely numb, as the Smoke Keeper grabbed both Alejandro and me by the arms.

"Now for the two of you."

We sat at the back of the black ship, helpless as it sailed across the Mire, headed for the Wall.

The Smoke Keeper had tied our hands in front of us with rope. Although I faced him, I couldn't meet Alejandro's eye. I was too ashamed.

I failed, and now Jeremiah, Jonquil, Fleck, Scape, and Alejandro will pay the price. I'm useless.

"I'm sorry."

My head whipped up. Alejandro looked miserable.

"Why are *you* sorry?" I whispered. This was all clearly my fault.

"Because it was my powers that got the sword melted. I used my good luck, and then the bad luck happened."

"It's my fault that you had to use your luck in the first place," I told him with a half smile. "I'm sorry too."

"What were you going to do with that sword, anyway? Just stab the Wall?"

"Sort of. It was going to have power in it, though."

"Power?"

"From the watch," I said. I felt in my pocket for the Smoke Ball and sighed with relief. It was still there. At least I hadn't lost that.

I could hear humming, and my head felt hazy. *We must be close to the Wall.*

I looked over the edge of the boat as we rode alongside the Wall, the mass of dark, luminous, swirling colors lighting our way.

Then the boat stopped.

"We've arrived," the Smoke Keeper announced.

I peered over the side of the ship and was met by the overwhelming glow of the Wall. I blinked away the brightness to see the colors of smoke swirled in a massive whirlpool—as if they were the fish in a feeding frenzy.

I leaned forward to get a better look. In the eye of the whirl was a face, thin and whittled away, but still recognizable. The Wall was sucking him in, but I could just make him out.

"Jeremiah."

"Where?" Alejandro followed my gaze, but then quickly turned back. I understood why. It wasn't a pretty sight. "Oh my" was all he said.

The Wall, it seemed, was eating Jeremiah. Ropes of smoke wrapped around his arms, legs, and neck, squeezing.

"Is he dead?" Alejandro asked.

"Not yet," I responded.

In the distance I could see another whirlpool. That had to be Jonquil. As horrible as I felt, I was relieved that I couldn't see his face too.

"I wanted you to see your friends before you joined them," the Smoke Keeper taunted as he crossed the ship to us, grinning broadly. Then he grabbed Alejandro by the shoulder.

"Please!" I tried to scramble up. *Not him.* "Just throw me in. He hasn't done anything wrong."

The Smoke Keeper shoved his face in mine. "No, child, I want you to watch and wait for your turn."

I could barely breathe as the Smoke Keeper dragged Alejandro, resisting against him, to the Wall.

"Ah, and it seems your little friends will be joining you soon as well." I looked out at what the Smoke Keeper was pointing at—the dot of Fleck's ship coming closer.

Stop, I wanted to scream at them, *run away.* But it

was too late. I had the Smoke Ball but not the sword.

I felt the warm surface of the Smoke Ball and had a realization: *I still have the watch.*

"Look here, girl! You don't want to miss this."

I dug my fingernail into the surface of the Smoke Ball as hard as I could, going over the lines to ensure they remained. Then I drew on it, blindly, as I watched the Smoke Keeper throw Alejandro into the Wall.

"Rose!" he shouted before being sucked in.

I couldn't respond, too focused, unwilling to picture anything else but the image inside my head.

I can still save them. I have to.

"Now you."

There, the last line. Just as the Smoke Keeper leaned in to grab me, I felt the energy pour from the Smoke Ball, out of my pocket.

"What?" The Smoke Keeper backed away as it formed in my hand—a small dagger blade made of the same swirling, glowing energy as the Smoke Ball. Just large enough to fit in my fist.

"What is that?"

The Smoke Keeper tried to grab for it, but it flitted out of his hands, like an illusion.

I whipped the blade up, slicing though the binds around my wrists.

"No!" The Smoke Keeper lunged at me. I backed up toward the Wall, holding my breath as he pushed me toward it.

I heaved the blade behind me—straight into the Wall.

The Smoke Keeper shrieked, dropping to his knees. "What is that? What are you doing?"

I pushed harder. I could feel the energy of the Wall getting sucked into the blade.

"Rose!" That was Fleck's voice.

They made it.

I tried to stop, to turn and look, but the dagger was too powerful—devouring the Wall entirely.

And with every inch of smoke absorbed, the blade grew brighter and brighter until I could no longer see. And then, just when I thought it could take no more—

Boom.

I was thrown back, flying through the air.

Seconds before I struck the Mire, everything went dark.

THE SMOKE SETTLES

I gasped, sitting up.

My heart was beating so fast that it was hard to breathe, and my eyes watered from the bright lights. Was I dead?

I looked around and realized with relief that I was still in the nurse's office at school. I could see her back to me at her desk in the front room—she must have just let us sleep when she'd returned to her office and found the two of us on the cots. I flopped back down, exhausted.

Had I really used the watch like that? My eyes went wide. *Oh no, the watch.*

I reached in my pants pockets, felt all along my sweatshirt. It was gone.

Then all the other memories flooded back.

Alejandro fell into the Wall! I rushed to him, still lying in the bed opposite me.

"Alejandro, wake up, please wake up."

I slapped his cheek over and over and sighed heavily with relief when his eyes finally flitted open.

"Rose?" he wheezed.

I laughed. He was here. He'd made it. *That means they all did!* I bent down, hugging him tightly, feeling warmed when he hugged me back.

Then I heard movement up front—Fallon had come into the nurse's office and was saying something to her. The nurse nodded and pointed to where we were.

"Rose? Alejan—" She stopped when she saw me sitting on Alejandro's bed, my arms still around him. We broke apart.

"Um," Fallon said, blushing, "Mrs. Lee wanted to make sure you were all right. Lunch is almost over."

I smiled at her, jumping up. Now that Alejandro was awake, I felt like a million bucks.

But before I could say anything to her, Fallon's phone began to buzz.

"Oh, it's my mom—hold on." She seemed almost afraid to answer. "Hello?"

I could hear Mrs. Berg's happy tears through the phone. "Fal, honey, he's awake! Jeremiah's awake!"

"He is?" Fallon gasped.

I turned to Alejandro with a smile . . . only to notice that he was sitting there empty-handed. He didn't have the watch anymore either.

My smile fell.

It's really gone.

The rest of the week flew by. Everything went back to the way it was before—or almost everything. Jeremiah came back to school on Monday with a shaved head.

That wasn't the only thing different about him. The new Jeremiah was quiet and wanted absolutely nothing to do with me. That might have been the best thing to come out of the whole week.

Yup, everything in my life went back to normal— well, except I actually had a friend to sit with now.

Alejandro and I had been working on our game, which we named *The Thirteenth Hour*, every day at lunch. He said he thinks we'll have a prototype by next year, in seventh grade. I told him my father would be very happy about that for my future college career.

Oh, and Fallon actually started looking at me again. Maybe even more than she looked at Samantha Plank, which thrilled me . . . mostly because it did not thrill Samantha.

I guess the biggest change in my life was sleeping. I hadn't been dreaming lately, not at all. I would stay up late, worried, wondering what had happened to them—Jonquil, Scape, and Fleck. Would I ever see them again?

It had all been real, I was sure of that, but the lingering memories of it seemed so . . . I don't know, *fake*, you know? Like I could never prove it to anyone or myself as anything more than a handful of very unsettling dreams.

If only I had Jo to talk to about it all . . .

I lay back on my bed, thinking about her for about the hundredth time. She still hadn't reappeared or even contacted anyone.

At the knock on my door, I sat up.

"Rose?"

"Yeah?"

It was Mom. She cracked open the door.

"Something came for you in the mail."

"Who's it from?" I asked, getting up to retrieve the plain white envelope from her.

"It's weird, there's no name on the return address." Then she winked at me, like she knew something, before shutting the door again behind her.

Strange.

But when I looked down at the envelope, my heart nearly stopped.

That's Jo's handwriting.

I ripped the letter open. At first I thought there was nothing inside.

Is this some sort of joke?

But then I turned the envelope upside down and shook it.

Something small fell out. I bent down to the carpet and scooped it up, holding it up to the light.

It was a single gold petal from the watch. I flipped it over and saw the carving of a fairy-tale castle on the other side.

Could it be?

I held the petal to my chest, and sure enough, it was still warm. She had given the world back to me.

I couldn't stop the smile from bursting across my cheeks.

Then I paused, a worry burning a hole in the pit of my stomach.

But the watch isn't mine. It never was. I remembered what Alejandro had said. What my great-great-grandfather had done.

This was his watch.

I felt the hole repaired by something: the excitement of returning the world to him. He could go on adventures of his own. Maybe he'd even take me to Eleven to see my friends, or Ten to see if that furry orange animal was still around.

As I picked up the envelope again, ready to drop the petal inside, a tiny scrap of paper peeked out.

With shaking fingers, I pulled it out and read what was on it:

You won't find me in the Thirteenth Hour anymore, Rose. Come and find me in another.

Yeah, I thought, lying back in bed again, giddy, *magic does exist, and we can still reach it.*

Acknowledgments

So, I told you all about Mrs. Spracher, right? Well, I only had so much room up there. I ought to tell you something else; two years later, my grandma Gayle, my mom, and I were sitting in a diner. Grandma Gayle said this: "Quinnie, if you become an author, you have to dedicate your first book to your mama, but you have to dedicate the second book to me."

Now, unfortunately, as lovely as Grandma Gayle is, she was two years too late, and I have but one second book to dedicate. That said, I *acknowledge* you instead . . . which, okay, isn't as good, but I did also put Globe, Arizona, in there (did you notice?). That's where Grandma Gayle lived my whole childhood, see, so now this book is for you, too, Grandma . . . even if you are a bit too slow.

But I should probably acknowledge some other folks: John Cusick and Liz Kossnar, for helping me cobble *The Thirteenth Hour* together, and Amanda Ramirez, for breathing life into it. I also would like to thank everyone who put their time into making this story into a real book, they are phantom hands working magic behind the scenes.

I can never forget Todd and Max, without whom I don't think I'd be writing at all.

And last of all, you. Thank you for dreaming with me and Rose for a while. We'll always be here should you need us.

(Also, remember that deal we made earlier. You have to write at least *two* books, because this is our contract and I will be waiting.)